Why hasn't Parker been chosen for the team?

"Listen to this, Foxy," Parker told his mare. "'The United States Equestrian Team is pleased to announce that Lyssa Hynde and her horse, Soldier Blue, have been added to the short list of horses and riders for the Olympic Games eventing team.'"

"Do you believe that?" he asked, waving the magazine at Foxy, who snorted and backed up. "Lyssa and Blue are going to the Olympics," Parker told her. He reached up to pat Foxy on the neck. "But what about us?"

Collect all the books in the Thoroughbred series

Collect all the books in the Ashleigh series

* coming soon

THOROUGHBRED

TEAM PLAYER

CREATED BY

JOANNA CAMPBELL

WRITTEN BY

ALICE LEONHARDT

HarperEntertainment

An Imprint of HarperCollinsPublishers

HarperEntertainment

An Imprint of HarperCollins*Publishers*
10 East 53rd Street, New York, NY 10022-5299

This is a work of fiction. The characters, incidents, and dialogues are products of the author's imagination and are not to be construed as real. Any resemblance to actual events or persons, living or dead, is entirely coincidental.

Produced by 17th Street Productions, an Alloy Online, Inc., company

HarperCollins books are available at special quantity discounts for bulk purchases for sales promotions, premiums, or fund-raising. For information please call or write: Special Markets Department, HarperCollins Publishers Inc., 10 East 53rd Street, New York, NY 10022. Telephone: (212) 207-7528. Fax: (212) 207-7222.

ISBN 0-06-106825-X

HarperCollins®, 📖 ®, and HarperEntertainment™ are trademarks of HarperCollins Publishers Inc.

Cover art © 2001 by 17th Street Productions, an Alloy Online, Inc., company

First printing: December 2001

Printed in the United States of America

Visit HarperEntertainment on the World Wide Web at www.harpercollins.com

❖ 10 9 8 7 6 5 4 3 2 1

"KAITLIN, QUIT DUCKING TO THE RIGHT OVER YOUR JUMPS!" Parker Townsend hollered. He was standing in the middle of Whisperwood Farm's outdoor ring, his hands shoved in the pockets of his goose-down vest. A chill wind was blowing, and dark clouds covered the late afternoon sun. "Walk Sterling and bring her in here!"

Kaitlin Boyce sat deep in the saddle and slowed the gray Thoroughbred mare to a walk. She and Sterling Dream were getting ready for their first preliminary event together. All winter Parker had been giving Kaitlin and several other riders lessons. Usually he enjoyed the lessons, but Kaitlin hadn't shown up on time for hers, and now Parker was running late.

Kaitlin halted Sterling in front of Parker. Tipping

1

back the brim of his baseball cap, he looked up at her. "Ducking isn't going to hurt you over these schooling jumps," he said. "But you've got to be more balanced when you do cross-country, or you and Sterling are going to get in trouble at Lexington Farms."

Kaitlin blew out her breath. "I don't know why I'm doing it."

"You're doing it because your right leg is stronger than your left, so you put more weight on your right stirrup," Parker explained.

"Really?" Kaitlin said. "Let me try that line of fences again."

Kaitlin was a hardworking student, and Parker was about to give in, but then he remembered that he'd promised to eat dinner with Christina and her family at Whitebrook Farm before he went to his world history class at the University of Kentucky. Parker hadn't seen his girlfriend, Christina Reese, since she returned from New Orleans, where Wonder's Star had won the Louisiana Derby.

Parker shook his head. "Sorry, I can't. Besides, Sterling's had enough jumping, and you can work on strengthening that left leg on your own." Raising his leg, he flexed his ankle. "Stand on the edge of a step. Put your weight on your left leg and push yourself up and down. Twenty times every time you use the stairs.

2

Now, I gotta go. See you Thursday afternoon for your lesson," he added, striding quickly across the ring before Kaitlin could ask him any more questions.

When he reached the gate, a group of young riders was leading their horses from the barn.

"Parker, can you give me a leg up?" one of the girls asked.

"Parker, is Jelly Roll's girth twisted?"

"Parker, is my bit adjusted right?"

"Parker . . ."

Parker sighed. "Where's Sam?" he asked, referring to Samantha Nelson, who owned Whisperwood with her husband, Tor Nelson. "Isn't she teaching your lesson?"

The little girl holding Jelly Roll nodded emphatically. "Yes, but can't you help us?" Parker glanced at Jelly Roll, a small pony who had his ears pinned because his girth *was* twisted. "All right. Just until Sam gets—"

"Parker, just the person I need," Samantha said as she strode from the barn, a gust of wind lifting her long auburn curls. "Will you set up a few low cross rails for us? Thanks."

Parker opened his mouth to tell her he didn't have time, but Sam had already turned her attention to the four riders. "Now, who needs a leg up, and *what* is wrong with Jelly Roll's girth?" she said.

Snapping his mouth closed, Parker spun on his boot heels and hiked back into the ring. Since working at Whisperwood paid for Foxy's board and his lessons, he couldn't afford not to help when Samantha asked. But lately, it seemed, that was all he did. And picking out hooves, tacking up reluctant ponies, and raking aisles wasn't getting him any closer to realizing his dream of being chosen for the Olympic eventing team.

By the time Parker had lowered the fences, the riders were finishing their warm-up stretches. Parker jogged from the ring. He'd have to hurry if he wanted to gallop Foxy before it got dark.

Foxy had been turned out all day in the pasture, which meant she'd be filthy, but Parker didn't believe in keeping the mare cooped up. He was sure that was the reason Foxy had stayed sound and sane in a sport that required tremendous athletic ability and heart.

Foxy had all of that and more, Parker thought proudly as he hurried out to the pasture. Four months ago he and Foxy had placed second at their first four-star three-day event. Four stars meant that Deer Springs was a top competition, and several members of the Olympic selection committee had been there. Afterward Parker had felt certain that he would be added to the United States Equestrian Team's list of horses and riders considered for the Olympic team. When no one contacted him, he was totally puzzled. How could the committee have overlooked their performance?

A high-pitched whinny interrupted his thoughts, and Foxy trotted to the gate. Parker couldn't help but admire the well-built, powerful mare. Foxglove was English-bred. Parker's grandfather, Clay Townsend, had bought her at an auction four years ago. Since then, they had trained hard at a sport where few made it to the top without serious injury or lack of success.

And as far as Parker was concerned, the Olympics *was* the top—and he was determined to get there.

"That means a solid gallop today," Parker told the mare as he slipped a halter over her muzzle and buckled it. "No more leisurely hacks. Rolex is only three weeks away."

Rolex would be their second three-day event. It was also rated four stars and attracted the best international talent. "If you want to get noticed by the Olympic selection committee," Samantha had told him, "you and Foxy have to do well at Rolex."

Three weeks seemed like forever. But at least five months were needed to condition a horse for the intensity of a three-day event. Parker had intentionally kept Foxy's workouts slow and easy, gradually adding gallops to increase her stamina. His patience had paid off. Not only was Foxy fit, but she looked forward to every ride.

Hooking the mare in crossties, Parker began the

messy job of knocking the mud off her coat. After a good curry, he pulled out the new horse vacuum that Tor had bought Sam for Christmas. Foxy eyed it warily.

"Quit being such a flake," he told her. "I've vacuumed you at least a dozen times." Turning it on, he let Foxy get used to the noise, then he ran the brush lightly down her neck.

Ten minutes later she was presentable enough to ride. Parker was tacking her up when Tor led a huge, big-footed Clydesdale-Thoroughbred cross named Bentley down the aisle. "Are you galloping Foxy now?" Tor asked.

Parker nodded. He slipped the bit into Foxy's mouth, then turned to stroke Bentley on his white blaze. The gelding had the coloring and height of a Clydesdale, but he wasn't as big-boned. "How's he doing?" he asked.

Tor was training Bentley for Brent Anderson, the gelding's owner. Brent only rode once a week and wanted his mounts perfectly trained for his outing.

"He's a gentle giant," Tor said. "But he needs to learn to gallop with some company."

"Foxy'll give him a workout," Parker said.

He saddled Foxy, then exchanged his baseball cap for his riding helmet. After giving her run-down bandages one last check, he led her from the barn. Tor was trotting Bentley in the cross-country field. Throwing up her head, Foxy whinnied excitedly when she saw him.

Parker pulled down his stirrups and mounted, barely landing in the saddle before Foxy took off. As she jogged through the gate, Parker gathered his reins and found his stirrups. Parker loved Foxy's energy and spirit. They were a perfect match.

For the past month Samantha had been pushing Parker to buy another horse. "In case Foxy gets injured," she said. "Plus you need to be bringing on a youngster."

Parker knew that all the top riders had a string of horses. Eventing was notoriously difficult. During the last Olympics, many horses had been withdrawn due to injuries.

The problem was, Parker knew he'd never find another horse as bold, sound, and sane as Foxy. So far, the horses he'd looked at in his price range had been too timid, too lame, or too crazy.

"I can see Foxy's going to be a great role model for Bentley," Tor joked when the gelding trotted up to Foxy.

"Think you two can keep up?" Parker asked as they did a warm-up trot along the fence line. He checked the stopwatch on his wrist. "We're going to gallop easy. Four hundred meters per minute."

Tor grinned. He'd shortened his stirrups and was

sitting like a steeplechase jockey. "We'll keep up."

"Then let's go." Parker touched his heels to Foxy's sides, and she leaped into a canter. They headed up the hill, Tor and Bentley beside them. Last fall, he and Sam had marked off a three-thousand-meter track around the field. Twice around was about the length of the cross-country portion of a three-day event. Once around was about the length of the steeplechase.

The sun was setting behind the hill, casting a golden glow on the fields. Even though Foxy was hyper, she quickly settled into a smooth lope. She had learned from experience to conserve her energy. As they cantered up and down the rolling hills, Parker balanced lightly in the saddle, his weight on his heels. Rhythm was essential for a great performance in the first phases of a three-day.

Bentley kept pace beside them, his hooves pounding the earth. But when they circled back toward the barn, Bentley's sides were heaving, and Parker could see that the gelding was too tired to continue.

Slowing Bentley, Tor touched his crop to his helmet. Parker saluted back, then checked his watch. Foxy wasn't even breathing hard, so he squeezed his calves, urging her to go faster. He'd gallop her a thousand meters more, this time at five hundred meters per minute. Then Parker would check Foxy's pulse and respiration to see how she was handling the pace.

Leaning forward, Parker clucked to Foxy. The mare flicked her ears, then lengthened her stride. The cold wind stung Parker's cheeks; adrenaline coursed through his body. He could see why Christina and her cousin Melanie loved racing so much. It was exhilarating.

When they reached the thousand-meter mark, Parker slowed Foxy to a walk, jumped off, and pulled his equine stethoscope from his jacket pocket. As Foxy walked in a tight circle around him, he pressed the stethoscope to her chest. Thirty-five beats a minute. Perfect.

Halting, Parker listened to Foxy's breathing and watched her heaving rib cage. She was already down to twelve breaths a minute. Parker laid his palm on her chest. It was only slightly damp.

He grinned. "Great job." When he stuck the stethoscope back in his pocket, he pulled out a Polo mint, Foxy's favorite. She lipped it daintily, worked it behind her bit, then crunched it between her back teeth. Parker ran his hands down her legs, checking for heat. The tendons were tight and cool.

"If we keep this up, you'll be unstoppable at Rolex," Parker told her. As he loosened the girth and ran up his stirrups, he thought about the event, which was held at the Kentucky Horse Park in Lexington. Rolex served as the primary USET selection trial. An array of Olympic officials would act as ground jury and technical delegates. The cross-country course was the toughest in the United States, and they'd be competing against horses and riders from all over the world. But if Parker wanted to get noticed, he and Foxy had to shine.

That was no problem. As far as Parker was concerned, Foxy was the most talented event horse *anywhere*.

When they reached the barn, Parker checked his watch. It was after five. The only problem with the weekly gallops was the long cool-down process afterward. He'd be late for dinner with Christina.

Parker led Foxy down the aisle. Chattering voices filled the barn. The younger riders had finished their lessons and were grooming their mounts. Samantha and Tor were standing by the tack room door, looking at a horse magazine. When Samantha spotted Parker, she whipped it behind her back.

"What's that?" Parker asked. Halting Foxy, he tried to peer around Samantha's back.

"Nothing!" Samantha said, smiling innocently.

"Uh, I've got to start bringing in the horses," Tor said, and hurried away down the aisle.

"What's going on?" Parker unsnapped his helmet and took it off. Even though the weather was cold, his hair was plastered to his head with sweat.

"Nothing, really." Samantha backed toward the tack room door.

Parker frowned. Samantha was a terrible fibber. "Yeah, right. Let me see what you're hiding." Reluctantly, Samantha brought her arm forward. She was holding a new issue of *USCTA*, the journal put out by the United States Combined Training Association.

Parker raised an eyebrow.

"All right, I might as well show you," Samantha said. "You'll find out sooner or later. There's an article about Lyssa Hynde and Soldier Blue."

"That's great." Parker wasn't surprised. Lyssa and Blue had won first place at the Deer Springs three-day event. When Parker first met Lyssa, he'd been jealous of the attention she'd gotten for her unorthodox riding style. Later, when Lyssa had helped him work with Foxy, he'd grown to admire her.

"Uh, you'd better read it." Opening the magazine, Samantha handed it to Parker. On one side of the spread there was a photo of Lyssa jumping Blue over a huge fence. Blue wore no bridle, and Lyssa was riding bareback.

"Nice picture," Parker commented.

"The article's good, too. Let me know what you think," Samantha said before disappearing into the tack room.

As Parker walked Foxy to her stall, he skimmed the

11

article. "'Lyssa and Soldier Blue, recent winners of the four-star Deer Springs three-day event, placed first at the Rocky Mountain one-day event in Colorado Springs,'" Parker mumbled to himself as he read. "'The win did not go unnoticed by Captain Mark Donnelly, the chef d'equipe of the United States Equestrian—'" Suddenly Parker stopped so abruptly that Foxy stepped on the back of his boot. Now he knew what Sam had been trying to hide from him.

"Listen to this, Foxy," Parker told his mare. "'The United States Equestrian Team is pleased to announce that Lyssa Hynde and her horse, Soldier Blue, have been added to the short list of horses and riders for the Olympic Games eventing team.'"

"Do you believe that?" he asked, waving the magazine at Foxy, who snorted and backed up. "Lyssa and Blue are going to the Olympics," Parker told her. He reached up to pat Foxy on the neck. "But what about us?"

2

ROLLING UP THE MAGAZINE, PARKER WHACKED IT ON HIS palm, a surge of anger filling him. Not because Lyssa and Blue had been put on the short list—they deserved it—but because he and Foxy hadn't.

Before now, the horses and riders selected had been big names such as David Breen, a former two-time gold medalist, and Nan Jenson, a silver medalist in the Pan American Games. As far as Parker knew, Deer Springs was the only four-star event in which Lyssa and Blue had competed. Why had the committee chosen them over Parker and Foxy?

Flipping the magazine back open, Parker read the rest of the paragraph. "'The USET has also awarded the pair a grant to train at the team's headquarters in New Jersey. Congratulations to Lyssa and Soldier Blue.'"

Parker clenched his jaw. He would have given anything to train in New Jersey under Captain Donnelly, the chef d'equipe for the United States Equestrian Team. His expertise was just what Parker and Foxy needed to make sure they made the team.

Foxy shoved Parker's shoulder, reminding him that she was itchy, hungry, and sweaty. "All right, all right," he grumbled. Throwing the magazine down, he undid the mare's girth and pulled off the saddle.

"So, what did you think about the article?" came a voice from the other side of Foxy. Parker didn't need to look over to know it was Samantha.

"I think it's great," Parker said, propping his saddle against the wall. "Lyssa deserves it."

"But?" Stooping, Samantha began taking off Foxy's run-downs.

"But why them and not us?" Parker asked, trying to sound as mature as possible under the circumstances.

Samantha shrugged. "I'm not sure. It may be your age; you're still young. Or maybe it's because you've only competed in one four-star—"

"But Lyssa's the same age as me, and she and Blue have only competed in one four-star, too," Parker cut her off. "Okay, so they *did* win. But we only missed first place by one knockdown."

Samantha handed him a dirty bandage and started

14

on the other leg. "That's true, but you haven't ridden in any international—"

"As far as I know, Lyssa hasn't done anything except that one-day mentioned in the article. So how did she get on the short list?" Parker continued. He pulled off Foxy's bridle and slipped on her halter. "In fact, according to Christina, all Lyssa's doing in Montana is herding *cows*. Has the USET started sponsoring calf roping?"

Samantha burst out laughing, and Parker frowned at her.

"What's so funny?" he demanded.

"*You*. You're having a tantrum. Like a two-year-old colt," Samantha said.

Parker propped his fists on his hips. "How am I supposed to react?"

"Well, instead of whining and complaining, you could be figuring out what *you* need to do to get on the short list."

Parker opened his mouth to argue with her but smiled sheepishly instead. "I guess I do sound like a big baby."

Samantha stood up and handed Parker another bandage. "Now, change of subject. Tomorrow morning I want you to go see another young horse with me."

Parker groaned. "No way. That last horse I tried out was part bucking bronco."

"I admit he was a little wild, but I promise, this one's big and handsome and a pussycat," Sam said.

"What's the catch?" Parker asked suspiciously.

"He's young and very green, so it'll take years before he can be ridden at the advanced level," Samantha said.

"What are they asking for him?" he said.

"Um . . . actually, Hap Palmer, the owner, hasn't told me the price," Samantha said quickly.

"Hap Palmer!" Parker groaned again. "But he's one of the best jumper trainers on the East Coast. Any horse of his will be way, way, *way* out of my league."

"You never know," Samantha said encouragingly. "Hap might need to sell the horse for some reason. Maybe he'll take payments."

Parker gave her a dubious look. "I doubt it. But okay, we may as well look at him," he said, his curiosity piqued. Maybe he would get lucky and find a terrific prospect he could actually afford.

Parker had never worried about money before. His parents, Brad and Lavinia Townsend, were the owners of Townsend Acres, one of the largest Thoroughbred racing operations in Kentucky, and they were one of the richest families in Lexington. But both his mother and father disapproved of eventing and had withheld all financial support "until you get some sense and start working at Townsend Acres," his father had declared.

But Parker refused to be blackmailed. Although he still lived at Townsend Acres, he was on his own financially. That was fine with him. He was determined to make it to the Olympics on his own.

"We can go to Hap Palmer's farm tomorrow," Parker said. "But then no more horse hunting until after Rolex. I need to concentrate on Foxy's training."

"Fair enough," Samantha said. "And remember what I said. Figure out what *you* need to do to get on that short list." When she left, Parker walked Foxy to the wash rack. He needed to hurry or else he'd never make it to Whitebrook for dinner.

As he adjusted the water temperature he thought how lucky he was to work for the Nelsons. Not only were they expert horse people, but whenever he felt discouraged, either Sam or Tor knew what to say.

An hour later Parker drove up Whitebrook's driveway toward the Reeses' clapboard farmhouse. Beyond the house, the farm's three barns and practice track were bathed in the glow of the vapor lights. Whitebrook wasn't the largest or the fanciest farm in Lexington, but its Thoroughbreds had an impressive record.

After hurrying up the sidewalk and up the steps to

the porch, Parker knocked on the front door. When Christina opened it, he grinned apologetically. "Sorry I'm late. My lesson ran over, I had to gallop Foxy and then bathe her, and she took forever to dry."

Christina turned around so quickly, Parker couldn't tell if she was annoyed or not. "You missed dinner, but I saved a plate of lasagna for you," she said, leading him into the kitchen.

Parker caught up with her and slipped his arm around her waist. Chris's reddish brown hair was up in a clip, and she was wearing a pretty purple sweater and black jeans. Parker wondered if she'd dressed up for his visit.

He ran his fingers through his own damp hair. He'd taken a fast shower at Whisperwood and thrown on the extra set of clothes he kept stashed in a gym bag in his truck. He wasn't exactly looking his best.

"You look good," he said. "Hey, this is the first time I've seen you in person since Star's win in the Louisiana Derby. Congratulations!"

Christina beamed up at him happily. "Thanks. Star was amazing."

"How's he doing since the race?" Parker asked, leaning against the kitchen counter.

"He's coming back slowly," Christina said as she turned on the microwave. "He's sound and in good spirits, but he lost weight from the stress of the long van ride home and the heat and humidity in Louisiana. It was worth it, though," she added. She handed him the front page of the *Racing Reporter*, a journal covering Thoroughbred racing in Kentucky. "Look at this."

"'Wonder's Star Is Sky High,'" Parker read the headline aloud. "'By Brynn Howard.' Isn't she the reporter who interviewed you before you went to New Orleans? The one who wrote that awful piece, 'Wonder's Star Has Fallen'?"

The microwave dinged. Christina took out the plate of lasagna and handed it to Parker. "Yup. Same one," she said. "She was so sure Star would never win another race. Now she's learned her lesson."

Parker munched on lasagna and skimmed the article. Then he glanced over at Christina, wondering when he should tell her the news about Lyssa Hynde and Blue being picked for the short list. Several months ago Christina and Star had spent a week in Montana at the Hyndes' ranch, and Chris and Lyssa had grown to be good friends. He would have to choose his words carefully, since he didn't want Christina to guess how jealous he was of Lyssa's success.

"Great article," Parker said. Holding up the paper, he read the last line of the article: "'Looks like the Kentucky Derby *is* on the menu for Wonder's Star.'"

19

Christina smiled. "Now I just need to keep him healthy and happy." Her smile faded. "You seem kind of down, Parker. Anything wrong with Foxy? Are you still riding in that one-day at Lexington Farms?" she asked.

"Foxy's doing great. And the one-day should be a breeze. I'm just doing it to sharpen her up for Rolex." Parker ate another bite, then pushed away his plate.

Christina looked at him expectantly.

"Okay, I guess I am a little down," Parker finally admitted. "I found out Lyssa and Blue are on the short list for the Olympics."

A grin spread over Christina's face. "But that's awesome!"

"For *her*, but not for *me*." Parker knew that Samantha would say he still sounded like a little kid, but he couldn't help it.

"No, that's good news for you, too," Christina said. "It means the committee is still selecting candidates. And that they're looking at young riders."

Parker frowned. He wished he could be as optimistic as Christina. "Okay, yeah. I guess. But what I can't figure out is why they only picked Lyssa and not me, too."

"Maybe they will pick you," Christina reassured him. "It's still early."

"No, it's not. In fact, I figure Rolex is my *last* chance to get noticed by the selection committee!" Parker said

20

tensely. "Sure, Foxy's doing great, but a thousand things could go wrong at Rolex. She could throw a shoe. We could go off course. I could fall off."

"Nothing will go wrong," Christina said. "You've got to have faith in yourself—and Foxy."

Parker shook his head. Christina sounded just like Samantha. Neither understood the pressure he would be under these next few weeks. He glanced down at his watch, suddenly realizing how late it was. His world history class started in half an hour.

"Sorry, Chris. I gotta run. My class starts at seventhirty. But thanks for dinner."

"Wait, Parker." Christina followed him down the hall. "How come you're always rushing around like crazy?"

When Parker reached the front door, he turned to face Christina. "Well, on top of worrying about getting on the Olympic team, I owe Tor for last month's board, and Samantha keeps harping on me to buy another horse. Where am I going to get money for a new horse? I had to scrape together the entry fee for Lexington Farms and Rolex. And I still haven't figured out how I'm going to pay for my expenses while I'm there."

"Why don't you ask your parents for help?" Christina suggested.

Parker stared at Christina as if she were crazy. "No way. You of all people know what my parents are like."

Christina crossed her arms in front of her chest. "But they *are* your parents. And they were proud of you after Deer Springs."

Parker snorted. "Until they found out no one from the Olympic selection committee asked me to be on the team."

Christina sighed in frustration. "Okay, maybe that was a dumb suggestion, but I'm just trying to help. I don't know. It seems like being chosen for the short list has taken over your life. It's like it's *you* against the world."

Parker rubbed his temples. He was getting a splitting headache, and he still had to sit through three hours of class. "Sorry," he muttered. "I don't mean to be such a jerk."

Christina looked away. Her arms were still crossed in front of her. *No wonder*, Parker thought. Christina had been trying to help, and all he'd done was argue with her. He touched her on the cheek. "I'll call you tonight after class. Maybe we can do something fun this weekend."

Christina shook her head. "You're going to Lexington Farms, remember?"

"Oh, right." There was a long silence. "Uh, maybe you can come along. You can help me with all the Whisperwood students. Most of them have never evented, so it will be crazy. If you come, at least we'd be together."

"But I'm racing one of our fillies on Saturday," Christina said, her tone flat. "Remember?"

"Sure, I remember," Parker said quickly, but when he couldn't meet Christina's gaze, he knew she knew he *hadn't* remembered.

Are things changing between us? Parker wondered. For the past few weeks he and Chris had been gradually drifting apart. First they'd argued about Christina's decision not to go to college. Then Christina had been really busy getting Star ready for his next race. And with Lexington Farms and Rolex coming up, there'd even be less time to spend together.

"Well, I've got to get to class," Parker said, turning to go out the door. "I'll call you tomorrow, okay?"

"Okay, bye," Christina said, closing the door abruptly behind him.

What a lousy way to end the evening, Parker thought as he walked to his truck. He felt completely drained. And not just from arguing with Christina.

Parker visualized his last bank statement. Did he have enough money to cover everything for Lexington Farms? And after that, how was he going to pay expenses at Rolex? And where was he supposed to get money for a new horse?

When he reached the university, he parked in the student lot. He was ten minutes early. Pulling his history notebook from his backpack, he opened it to the previous week's notes on economics in ancient Greece. He needed to review before class, but he couldn't stop thinking about his money problems.

Samantha was right. If he was going to be a serious eventer, he needed to be bringing along a second horse. He also needed to find a way to pay for his expenses so that he could concentrate on doing well at Rolex, or he might as well kiss the Olympics good-bye. However, figuring out how to come up with the money was giving him a major headache.

Christina was right. The only option was to ask his parents for help. After class he'd call Samantha and see if he could pick her up later the next day, around nine, to go see the horse at Hap Palmer's. That way he could have breakfast with his mom and dad and bring up the subject of money.

There was only one problem. He'd rather clean a thousand stalls than ask his parents for money.

Parker sighed as he shut the notebook.

Too bad he didn't have any other choice.

"Parker!" Lavinia Townsend's shrill voice rang up the stairs. "Are you coming down to have breakfast with us?"

Parker groaned and rolled onto his back, one arm flung across his face. How did his mother even know he was home? They hadn't been around when he came home from class the night before. And usually he was gone in the mornings before they woke up.

"Be right down," Parker called. Throwing back the covers, he sat up and rubbed his palm across his whiskery chin. Then he slipped on clean jeans and a T-shirt and ran his fingers through his hair, trying to smooth it down.

His mother and father hated to see him looking scruffy. If he wanted their help, he'd have to make an effort. But at the same time he didn't want to look too polished, or they'd know he was up to something.

When he entered the dining room, his parents were sitting at one end of the long mahogany table. Crystal goblets were filled with orange juice, croissants were arranged on a silver tray, and a buffet had been set up on the sideboard.

His father was seated at the head of the table, reading the newspaper. Next to him, his mother chatted away, oblivious to the newspaper in front of her husband's face. Both were dressed in tailored suits, as usual.

"Good morning, Mother, Father," Parker said, walking over to the buffet table. At the sight of all the food—fresh fruit, scrambled eggs, sausage, new potatoes—his stomach growled noisily. Picking up a serving spoon, he scooped up some scrambled eggs and ate them ravenously.

His mother arched one perfectly plucked brow. "There are plates and silverware, Parker. Or are you pretending to be a starving vagrant?"

Parker stuffed a sausage in his mouth. He heard the newspaper rustle.

"Really, son. You know we don't wear jeans at breakfast. Don't you think it's time you dropped the rebellious act?"

Grabbing a plate, Parker filled it with food, his back to his parents. As always, everything he did was wrong in their eyes, and everything his mother and father said made him angry. But if he was going to ask for help, he had to play nice.

"Foxy and I are competing at Lexington Farms on Saturday," Parker said.

"That's nice," his father said. "And what are you competing for? Another trophy for your dresser?" Parker heard the sarcasm in his father's voice. "Too bad Foxy isn't a racehorse. At least then she'd be *making* money instead of *costing* money."

There it is, Parker thought ruefully. The same old conversation they'd been having for years.

"Now, Brad, not everything has to be about racing," his mother said. "But really, Parker, what *are* you living on these days? Why do you continue to pour your paycheck into that horse and that sport? You do get a paycheck from the Nelsons, don't you? It's hard to tell by looking at you. You don't even have any decent clothes."

Parker snorted. *Gee, thanks for defending me, Mother.* Turning, he scooped up more eggs, then sat down across the table from his mother. His father had gone back to reading the newspaper, as if bored with the conversation.

Parker took a deep breath before beginning to speak. "I've explained all this before, Mother," he said patiently. "I love eventing as much as you and Dad love racing. I enjoy working at Whisperwood—"

Abruptly Brad shut the newspaper. "There is no future in eventing! Samantha and Tor Nelson are perfect examples. They work night and day and have nothing to show for it. I bet they're not even paying you. You're just too proud or too thickheaded to admit it."

Parker bristled. It was one thing to berate him—he was used to it—but he wasn't going to let his father criticize Sam and Tor.

"The Nelsons are two of the finest people I know," Parker declared. "Sure, they work hard, but they love what they do."

"Loving what you do wears off fast when you're fifty years old and still mucking out stalls." Brad shook one finger in the air. "Twenty years from now, they'll still be exactly where they are now."

Parker's jaw tightened. "You mean they won't have a mansion, five barns, twenty employees, and a bank account full of money, like you?"

"My point exactly!" Brad replied, a note of triumph in his voice.

Parker stood up so fast, his chair tipped backward. "No, *my* point exactly. If success means being like you and Mother, I'd rather be Sam and Tor any day."

"Parker!" his mother exclaimed, a shocked expression on her face.

"Now if you'll excuse me." Tossing down his linen napkin, Parker stormed out of the dining room. "I've got work to do—at that dump, Whisperwood."

"Parker, you didn't finish your breakfast," his mother called.

"Oh, let him go," Parker heard Brad grumble. "One day the boy will wake up and see that we're right. If only he'd gone to that business school in Italy, we wouldn't be dealing with this eventing nonsense."

Parker leaped up the stairs. He'd heard enough.

He'd been delusional to think his parents would help him out.

He was on his own.

3

"SUNNY DAY IS THREE YEARS OLD," SAMANTHA WAS TELLING Parker as they drove down Interstate 75. The trip to Sun Hill, Hap Palmer's farm, took about an hour each way, so Parker was glad he'd left breakfast in such a rush and picked Samantha up early.

"He's about sixteen-three hands, charcoal gray with great jumper bloodlines," Samantha continued. "I saw him last fall, and he was pretty gawky. By now he's probably muscled out. I bet he'll be ready for the novice level next spring."

"So why's Hap selling this wonder horse?" Parker asked. His gut told him that the trip to Sun Hill was a waste of time. If the colt was half as nice as Samantha said, Parker wouldn't be able to afford him anyway.

"My friend Juanita, who works for Hap, said he

29

owns too many horses. He's concentrating on training and showing horses for clients. That's where the money is."

It certainly isn't in eventing, Parker started to say, but caught himself when he realized he sounded just like his father.

"But why is Hap selling Sunny Day? Is he blind in one eye? Clubfooted?"

Samantha shot him an amused look. "Always the skeptic, huh?"

"That's me." Parker thought back to the previous night's argument with Christina. He'd definitely been on the negative side. And later, when he called her after his class, she'd sounded distant. But she had every right to be. Parker *hadn't* been much fun lately.

"There's the sign for Sun Hill," Samantha said. "Take the next right."

Parker steered the truck into a paved driveway lined with pine trees and white fences. To the right of the drive was a large arena filled with an impressive display of Prix de Nations–size jumps. To the left was a huge barn connected to an indoor arena by a covered walkway. Everything was freshly painted and spotless.

"Look, there's Sunny Day," Samantha exclaimed, pointing past Parker. "He really has filled out."

Slowing the truck, Parker glanced out the driver's-side window. Someone was lunging a dappled gray horse in a paddock. The horse's neck was arched and his tail was raised like a flag. He had a long and springy stride, powerful haunches, and a strong, sloping shoulder.

Parker caught his breath. If that *was* Sunny Day, he was magnificent.

He glanced over at Samantha, who was grinning at him. "Nice, huh?" she said.

"More than nice," Parker replied. "But we'd better take a closer look to make sure one of his legs isn't wooden," he teased.

"He's sound," Samantha assured him. "That's my friend Juanita lunging him. She's been working for Hap for the past year. She's the one who told me about him."

They parked and jumped out of the truck. As they approached the paddock, Samantha waved at Juanita.

"Whoa," Juanita told the big gray colt. Instantly Sunny Day halted and faced her, his ears pricked at attention.

"You weren't lying," Samantha told her friend. "He is one handsome colt."

Samantha introduced Parker to Juanita, who immediately handed the lunge line to him. "Why don't you

31

lunge him?" she said. "He's totally voice-trained."

"How is he under saddle?" Parker asked.

"Barely started," Juanita admitted. "We've lunged him with saddle and bridle, and I've been on his back. Hap just has too many horses and not enough time." Turning, she stroked the gelding's muzzle affectionately. "But Sunny's been a real sweetheart, haven't you, boy?"

Parker took the lunge line and led the colt into the middle of the paddock. He didn't want to get his hopes up, but if Sunny was that green, he might be affordable.

For the next ten minutes Parker lunged the young gelding, even trotting him over a small crossbar. Sunny tucked his front legs and arched his back as if it were a four-foot parallel.

Parker couldn't help it. He was impressed. Halting the colt, he walked around him, inspecting him from every angle. He couldn't find a single thing wrong with him.

"So you like my horse?"

Parker glanced over his shoulder. A small man with a wiry build wearing breeches and tall boots had walked into the paddock. Parker recognized him from photos in *Practical Horseman* magazine. It was Hap Palmer.

Parker stuck out his hand. "Yes, sir. I like your colt a lot. Did you breed him on the farm?"

Ignoring Parker's proffered hand, Hap nodded. "He's out of Sunny Lady, the mare I rode in the 1980 Olympics."

Parker's eyes practically bugged out. He bit the inside of his cheek to keep his mouth from hanging open. He didn't want Hap to think he was totally starstruck.

"Have any of Sunny Lady's foals gone into three-day eventing?" Samantha asked.

Hap raised his eyebrows as if Sam had said a dirty word. "No, but I have the utmost confidence that they could handle any sport, even eventing."

Parker wasn't sure if Hap's answer was a put-down or if the guy just didn't know much about eventing. He also wasn't sure how to bring up the subject of money. Obviously, most of Hap's clients didn't have to worry about such mundane problems.

Fortunately, Samantha came right to the point. "How much are you asking?"

"Fifty thousand, which is a bargain for such a fine colt," Hap said.

Parker's mouth went dry. Maybe it *was* a bargain for Hap's usual clients. To Parker, fifty thousand dollars might as well have been a million.

Hap must have noticed Parker's glum expression, because he nodded brusquely. "If you have any questions, I'll be in the barn office."

"Yeah, I have a question for you," Parker muttered when Hap was out of earshot. "Are there any banks nearby that I can rob?"

Samantha and Juanita overheard and laughed. "Sorry about that, guys," Juanita apologized. "I really didn't know how much he was asking for the colt."

"Not your fault." Samantha patted her friend on the shoulder. "Sunny's everything you said he was. So is Hap," she added under her breath.

"You mean I wasn't the only one who thought he was arrogant?" Parker asked. Actually, Hap and his dad had a lot in common.

Juanita shrugged. "He has clients from all over the world waiting in line for his training expertise *and* his horses."

"Well, I hope this guy goes to a great home." Parker sighed.

Juanita took the lunge line from Parker. "So what is your price range?" she asked him.

Pulling his billfold from his back pocket, Parker opened it and looked inside. "About twenty dollars?"

"Don't listen to him," Samantha said. "He knows he's not going to find anything halfway decent for under five thousand."

Juanita tapped her lip with one finger. "Sam says you're a terrific rider with a terrific way with horses *and* you're not afraid of anything."

"Aw, gee, Sam said all those nice things about me?" Parker said in a mock bashful voice.

"Would you like to look at another horse?" Samantha asked. "One that would be in your price range? I'm telling you, he would be the *ultimate* challenge."

"That sounds intriguing. What horse are you thinking about?" Samantha asked.

Without answering, Juanita led Sunny from the paddock. Parker and Samantha exchanged glances.

"Coming, Parker?" Samantha called. She was walking beside Juanita toward a run-in shed.

Parker hurried after them to another field, which was hidden by a stand of pines. Several horses grazed in the pasture. It took only one glance for Parker to see that these were not the pampered colts in Sunny Day's field. These horses had shaggy, dirt-crusted coats, as if they'd been turned out all winter without blankets.

"Is this the Sun Hill Retirement Home for Horses?" he joked.

Juanita laughed. "Sort of. But the horse I want you to see is only eight years old." She pointed to a tall mahogany bay gelding with a strip of white down his nose and three white socks. "That's Ozzie."

Parker frowned as he studied the horse. Ozzie was

about seventeen hands, but from across the field he looked more like a plow horse than an eventing prospect.

"Uh, I know I can't afford much, Juanita, but I do need a horse who will be able to handle four-foot jumps with six-foot spreads."

"Ozzie can," Juanita said. "Believe it or not, that fuzzy mess of a horse is the Wizard of Oz."

Parker's brows shot up. "*The* Wizard of Oz?"

"The horse Hap rode in the Nations Cup?" Samantha exclaimed, sounding equally astonished.

Juanita nodded.

"What happened?" Samantha asked. "Why is he turned out with a bunch of old broodmares?"

Juanita set her arms on the top of the fence. "It's a long story," she said dramatically. Turning, she gazed directly into Parker's eyes. "One that I hope has a happy ending."

4

PARKER LOOKED BACK AT THE HORSE, TRYING TO IMAGINE the dirty, unimpressive-looking animal in the pasture as the sleek, powerful jumper he'd seen in photographs.

"As you know, the Wizard of Oz was Hap's top jumper," Juanita began. "He campaigned him hard for almost two years. The horse won hundreds of thousands of dollars in prize money. However, the Nations Cup was the last show where he won anything."

"Did he go lame?" Parker asked.

Juanita shook her head. "No. He's totally sound. Believe me, every vet on the East Coast checked him out."

"What happened?" Sam asked.

"Ozzie just quit. After the Nations Cup, Hap took him to one of the big indoor shows. Ozzie cantered into the arena and promptly refused the first jump three times. You can imagine how embarrassed Hap was, with clients and journalists watching. After that it got worse." Juanita shook her head. "I swear Ozzie could count. Every show, he refused the first jump three times, then turned and trotted toward the gate."

"Sounds like a smart horse," Sam said, as if she were impressed with Ozzie's bad behavior. "So what did Hap do?"

"He tried everything—supplements, blinders, massage, whips, equine therapists. He even consulted a horse psychic. But it only got worse. Soon Ozzie wouldn't even go in the arena. Now you can't come near him with a bridle or saddle. It was like he just decided he'd had enough. Not that I can blame him."

Sam and Parker were listening attentively.

"Hap pushes his horses," Juanita explained in a low voice. "Let's face it, prize money pays the bills. And competing in the top jumping competitions or as a team member draws more clients. The clients want fast results, and results mean winning." She shrugged. "Some horses can handle it. Others, like Ozzie, burn out."

38

"So Hap wants to sell Ozzie?" Samantha asked.

"He sold him once to some guy who wanted an instant junior jumper for his kid. But Ozzie wouldn't jump, and the buyer threatened to sue if Hap didn't take him back. Since Hap didn't want any more bad publicity, he turned Ozzie out. He's so disgusted with Ozzie's behavior, I bet he'd give him away."

"That sounds like my price range," Parker said wryly. "But what makes you think *I* can do anything with Ozzie?"

Juanita shrugged. "You'd be taking a gamble," she admitted. "But from what Sam says about you, you'd be the right person to do it. Ozzie needs a smart, experienced, strong rider—not a kid or a weekend hacker. And I bet he'd love cross-country."

"I don't know," Parker said doubtfully.

Just then the big horse ambled over, a tuft of hay hanging from his mouth. He stuck his head over the fence and tried to rub it against Parker's shoulder. When Parker scratched under the gelding's long forelock, Ozzie flapped his lips like an old school horse.

"It seems like a huge gamble," Parker said, shaking his head. "I realize he was once the Wizard of Oz, but now he looks like plain old Ozzie."

Climbing over the fence, Juanita slipped a halter on the horse's big head, then looped the lead line over his neck and tied the loose end to the other side.

"Get on," she told Parker. "You have to ride him bareback, since it's the only way he'll let you ride him these days. Get a feel for him and then tell me he doesn't have the potential."

Parker glanced at Samantha, who grinned back at him and shrugged. "It's worth a try," she said.

Reluctantly Parker climbed the fence. Juanita led Ozzie up beside him, and he swung onto the horse's back. Instantly Ozzie strode off.

"Ouch." Parker grimaced as he settled on the horse's backbone. "It's not exactly like sitting in an armchair."

He gathered up the lead line in his hands and sat deeper. Ozzie arched his neck and collected himself. His stride was smooth, and when Parker pressed his calves against one side or the other, the big gelding easily tracked right and left.

Parker was pleasantly surprised. The horse obviously remembered his training.

"He has fantastic gaits," Juanita called.

Parker squeezed Ozzie into a trot. His stride was long and springy with lots of impulsion, which was important for dressage. As they trotted around the band of broodmares, Ozzie showed off with an extended trot.

"Look at that extension!" Sam cried.

Suddenly Ozzie ducked his head, tearing the lead line from Parker's grasp, and began to buck. For a second Parker was so surprised, he almost lost his balance. Then he grabbed hold of a chunk of mane with one hand and used a pulley rein to pull the horse's head up. Ozzie bolted into a canter, and Parker let him go. They cantered across the field, and Parker grinned. The horse had incredible power and a smooth, ground-eating stride.

After slowing Ozzie to a walk, Parker patted the gelding's fuzzy neck. "You were right, Juanita," he gasped breathlessly when he halted and slid off. "The guy's an incredible mover. But I can't ride him in a pasture with a halter forever. And how will I get him to jump for me?"

"I don't know," Juanita said. "Like I said before, I'd love to see a happy ending to Ozzie's story. He's so talented, it would be a waste if he spent the rest of his life turned out with broodmares. Or was sold to someone who mistreated him," she added under her breath.

Parker looked at Samantha, who was sitting on the fence, scratching Ozzie's face. The big horse's eyes were half closed, and he let out a contented sigh.

"Why don't we ask Hap if you can take him for two weeks on trial?" Samantha suggested. "I bet Ozzie will

41

like Whisperwood, and maybe a change of scenery will help his attitude."

"First we need to ask Hap how much he wants for Ozzie," Parker said. "What if he's hoping Ozzie will be a Nations Cup winner again someday?"

"Trust me, Hap's given up on him," Juanita said.

Ten minutes later Parker and Samantha found Hap in his office. When they knocked, Hap motioned them in. He was talking on the phone.

Trying not to eavesdrop, Parker glanced around the office. Ribbons and trophies lined the walls along with photos of Hap mounted on beribboned horses or shaking hands with movie stars and political figures.

"What can I do for you?" Hap asked when he finally hung up.

"Juanita showed us Ozzie," Parker said.

"Ozzie?" For a second Hap seemed puzzled, and then he sighed and rolled his eyes. "Oh, you mean the Wizard of Oz. What about him?"

"We'd like to know if he's for sale, and if he is, we'd like to take him for a two-week trial," Samantha said.

Hap pressed his lips into a tight line. His phone rang, but he ignored it. "Juanita filled you in on his problems, and you're still willing to try him out?"

"Yes, sir," Parker said.

"And you would be willing to sign a form stating

that I have not misrepresented the horse, and releasing Sun Hill and me from all liability?"

Parker nodded silently, although as he did so he wondered, *What in the world am I getting into?*

"Of course," Samantha agreed. "And since Ozzie would be staying at Whisperwood, I would like you to sign our standard contract as well."

Hap tipped his head in acknowledgment.

Parker shifted uncomfortably. "Uh, I'd also like to discuss a price. . . ."

Hap held his hand up. "*If* you and Ozzie make it through two weeks, and *if* you decide to buy him, we'll discuss terms. Fair enough?"

Parker opened his mouth to protest, but Hap cut him off. "Don't worry. I understand you have a price range, young man," he said. "Leave directions with Juanita and I'll have Ozzie delivered tomorrow morning. Now, if you'll excuse me." Picking up the phone, he turned his back on them.

Parker and Samantha hurried from the office. When they got outside, Parker exhaled loudly. "Wow. That guy really thinks he's king, doesn't he?"

Samantha chuckled. "You should be used to it. He reminds me of your father."

Juanita jogged up to find out what happened. "Well?" she said.

"Tomorrow Ozzie's coming to Whisperwood for a two-week trial," Parker told her.

"Yes!" Juanita cried. "I'll bring him over. Thanks, Parker," she added gratefully.

"For what?"

"For taking a chance with Ozzie," she said. "I know he isn't perfect like Sunny Day, and I know he'll be a handful, but if you stick with him, I don't think you'll regret it."

Parker smiled wryly. He tried to picture Ozzie competing cross-country at an event such as Rolex. But his mind was blank.

He sighed. "I hope I won't regret it, either."

Thursday morning Parker was washing Foxy after a lesson with Samantha when he heard the roar of a truck motor. Swinging around, he spotted a huge horse van rumbling up the drive toward the barn. Sun Hill Farms was printed in bold letters on the side.

"Ozzie's here," Parker called to Samantha, who was in the jumping ring, adjusting the fences for her lessons later on.

"I'll go tell Tor!" Sam called, and pointed to her husband, who was parking the tractor behind the barn. He'd been on the cross-country course replacing some broken rails.

Hurrying into the barn, Parker threw a cooler over Foxy. He could hear the van turning around in the driveway. A horse whinnied inside it, and Foxy whinnied back.

Parker's pulse quickened. He suddenly felt nervous about Ozzie.

He and Foxy had had a few problems, but they'd been in sync from the beginning. The mare's own spirited personality had instantly responded to Parker's devil-may-care riding style and attitude.

What if Ozzie and I don't mesh? Parker thought. Then he caught himself. Ozzie was a horse, not a girlfriend. Sure, there was extra pressure because Ozzie had once been famous. And Parker had only two weeks to make a decision about buying him. But if he decided he wouldn't be able to deal with the big horse and his problems, at least he'd be in good company. In reality, he had nothing to lose.

Striking the barn floor with an impatient hoof, Foxy reminded Parker to pay attention to her. "Hey, cool it," he told her affectionately. "After today's workout, you get to chill out until Saturday, when we go to Lexington Farms."

He led Foxy down the aisle to the open barn door. The van had parked, and Tor was talking to Juanita. A loud banging came from the back of the van.

"I'd better get him out before he tears the place apart," Juanita said.

"I'll put Foxy in her stall," Samantha said as she strode up the aisle. "You'd better welcome Ozzie to Whisperwood."

Parker handed her Foxy's lead and went outside. Tor and Juanita had lowered the side ramp, and Parker could see Ozzie's long head peering around the door frame. His shaggy forelock hung in his eyes, and there was a jagged scar above one nostril that Parker hadn't noticed before.

As Juanita led him down the ramp, Ozzie took hesitant steps, stopping halfway to view his new surroundings. Juanita had attempted to groom him and clip his ears and bridle path, but his coat was still fuzzy and dusty, his hooves needed trimming, and his muscles were slack from disuse.

He is definitely not handsome, that's for sure, Parker thought. But Tor, who was standing beside him, whistled with appreciation.

"So that's the Wizard of Oz, huh," Tor declared. "Look at that shoulder and those hindquarters. No wonder he could jump anything."

Parker squinted, trying to see Ozzie through Tor's eyes. Like Samantha, Tor had a knack for assessing a horse's potential, no matter what its condition. The two had bought many bargains that way.

"Where do you want him?" Juanita asked.

46

"We're going to turn him out with Toby, one of our lesson horses," Tor said.

Taking the lead from Juanita, Parker patted Ozzie on the neck. Just then Samantha came up, cooing as she stroked Ozzie's heavily whiskered muzzle.

"Any suggestions about what Hap did or didn't do, and what worked or didn't work?" he asked Juanita.

She rolled her eyes. "Do you have a couple of days?"

"Why don't you stay for lunch?" Tor suggested.

Juanita agreed, and Samantha and Tor guided her toward the house while Parker led Ozzie to a small pasture behind the barn. Ozzie walked with his head low and his ears cocked sideways as he gazed around. Nothing seemed to bother him, Parker noticed, probably because in his show-jumping career, Ozzie must have been everywhere and seen everything.

"How's this look?" Parker asked as he opened the gate into the pasture, which had an adjoining run-in shed. Toby glanced up from his grazing. "I know there aren't as many women to impress," Parker told Ozzie. "But then, there aren't as many women to pick on you, either," he added, noting the scratches and bite marks on Ozzie's flank.

He unhooked the lead line, and Ozzie ambled over

47

to Toby, who pinned his ears and moved away. After shutting the gate, Parker leaned on the fence. He hadn't expected Ozzie to suddenly turn into a fiery stallion, but it would have been nice to see some animation, or excitement, or . . . *something*.

Parker sighed. *Lexington Farms, Rolex, making the Olympic team, money. And now Ozzie.*

Just one more thing to worry about.

5

ON FRIDAY WHISPERWOOD WAS HUMMING WITH ACTIVITY as everyone got ready for Lexington Farms. Parker and Tor were both competing, along with a few of Whisperwood's students.

That morning Parker had only gotten to see Ozzie for a second, when he'd thrown the horses hay for breakfast. Now it was four in the afternoon and the lesson students had arrived, bringing their usual pandemonium. Parker was teaching Justin and Penny how to pull and trim the manes of their mounts, who were crosstied in the aisle. At the same time, he was trying to clip Foxy's bridle path and fetlocks.

"Not such a huge hunk, Justin," Parker said. "We want neat, not bald." Justin was ten years old, and he and his mount, Bouncer, were riding novice, which was the easiest level.

Taking a few strands of Bouncer's mane in his fingers, Parker demonstrated how much to pull. "Only do this where the mane is thick. Otherwise use the thinning shears and cut it, like this. But just a little at a time. No scalping."

Justin chuckled. "Hey, a bald horse would look cool."

"Uh, right." Parker headed down the aisle to where Foxy waited patiently.

"This short?" Penny called, holding up her hand and indicating an inch with her fingers. Parker did an about-face and went over to Chili, the large pony she would be riding the next day.

"No, that would be too short—Chili would have a Mohawk." Parker held up his own fingers. "About three inches. Then we can train it to lie flat. Maybe." He gave Chili's thick, springy mane a dubious look.

"Now, are you guys all set for now?" he asked them before turning the clippers on. "I have to get Foxy done."

He'd just started clipping her bridle path when he heard Sam call his name.

Parker switched off the clippers. "What?"

"Great news!" Samantha exclaimed as she stepped

around Foxy, a wide grin on her face. "Captain Donnelly called this morning."

Parker froze in place. "C-captain Donnelly?" he stammered.

"You know, the chef d'equipe for the USET?"

"I know who he is," Parker said. His heart was pounding wildly. There was only one reason Donnelly would be calling Whisperwood. *He wanted to tell Parker that he and Foxy had made the short list for the Olympic team!*

"Captain Donnelly called to ask if Jeff Steffen and Lyssa could board their horses at Whisperwood while they prepared for Rolex," Samantha continued. "Isn't that terrific?"

Parker stared at Samantha in disbelief. Had he heard her right?

"Lyssa and Blue are coming all the way from Montana," Samantha said, "and Jeff's coming from Vermont. They want to board and train here for two weeks before Rolex to get their horses acclimated."

As Samantha rattled on about Jeff and Lyssa, Parker wondered how he could have been such a fool. He should have known Captain Donnelly wouldn't be calling about him.

Crouching down, Parker grabbed a toothbrush from his grooming box and cleaned off the clipper blades.

Samantha touched Parker on the shoulder. "That means Captain Donnelly will be here at Whisperwood. He'll get to see you in action."

Parker looked up at her. "You mean Donnelly will be here to watch me blow it at Rolex."

"No, I didn't mean that at all," Samantha said firmly. "It will give Captain Donnelly a chance to get to know you. He'll see you ride lots of horses, teach lessons, work with the horses. It won't take him long to figure out what an asset you'd be for the team. Having Jeff and Lyssa at Whisperwood is a great opportunity."

Parker stood up. "Right. And Whisperwood will get tons of publicity," he said bitterly.

Samantha placed her fists on her hips. "It'll be good publicity for you, too. *If* you get that chip off your shoulder."

"Chip? What chip? That's a block of wood on my shoulder," Parker shot back, but then his mouth tilted up in a reluctant grin. "Okay. Anyway, it'll be good to spend time with Jeff and Lyssa," he said.

"Parker," Penny called, "will you check Chili's mane?"

"Just a minute!" Parker called back.

"I'm glad you like the idea," Samantha said, turning her attention to Justin and Bouncer. "How's the mane pulling coming?"

Deep in thought, Parker set down the clippers and walked over to help Penny. Samantha was right. Having Captain Donnelly around Whisperwood couldn't hurt. But at the same time, Parker was still disappointed that he hadn't made the short list. And he doubted that Captain Donnelly would change his mind after watching Parker teach a walk-trot lesson or get bucked off Ozzie.

He showed Penny how to wet Chili's mane and tame it flat. Then he went back to clipping Foxy. He was almost finished when Christina came into the barn. Parker wasn't sure why she was at Whisperwood, and he hadn't talked to her since their awkward conversation on Tuesday night.

"Hey," Parker said. "What brings you to Whisperwood?"

"Foxy looks terrific," Christina commented, stroking the mare's glossy neck before answering him. "I was hoping you'd have time to show me the new horse."

Parker unplugged the clippers and began to clean them off. For the first time in ages, he felt awkward around Christina. He hadn't even told her about Ozzie, but she must have found out from Sam. "You mean Ozzie?" he said.

"Yeah. Sam says he's pretty nice."

"It's hard to tell. I won't have time to do anything with him until this one-day is over." Setting the clippers in the box, he unsnapped Foxy from the crossties. "Let me put Foxy in her stall and I'll show him to you."

Minutes later Parker led Christina from the barn and around back.

Christina leaned over the board fence. "Where is he?" she asked, her head swiveling right and left as she looked everywhere except at the two horses grazing right in front of her.

Parker chuckled. Obviously, she was looking for Wizard of Oz, the horse who had won the Nations Cup. Leaning on the top board, he nodded at Ozzie. "Right there." With an amused expression, he watched Christina's eyes widen.

"Don't worry. I never would have guessed Ozzie was once a Grand Prix jumper, either," Parker said.

"Sam told me about his problems," Christina said. "Sounds like he'll be a challenge."

"*If* I buy him," Parker said, putting emphasis on the *if*. "Although Tor and Sam both love him already," he added, as if trying to justify why he was trying him out. "But if he doesn't work out, that's okay. I'm not in a hurry to get a new horse."

"But what if something happens to Foxy?" Christina asked, still watching Ozzie. She seemed to be avoiding Parker's eyes.

Parker shrugged. "I'd have to take some time off. I can't afford to buy a horse with Foxy's training. I can't even imagine what she's worth now. And even if Ozzie does work out, he won't be able to replace her for a long time. You know how long it takes to get a horse up to advanced-level competition."

"Actually, I don't," Christina said. "I was too impatient."

"No, you just decided you like racing better," Parker said.

Raising his head, Ozzie came over to the fence to say hello. He lipped at Christina's palm, searching for a treat. "He seems sweet," she said, scratching under his forelock.

Parker snorted. "As long as you're not asking him to do something he doesn't want to do. You should hear some of the stories Juanita told us. The last time Hap tried to ride Ozzie over a course, the horse flipped over."

Christina shuddered. "I hope he doesn't do that when you're on him."

"I wasn't sure you cared," Parker said without thinking.

Christina glanced sharply at him. "Wow, if you think that, then there really must be something wrong. It's not all in my head."

"You noticed, too, huh?" Parker said soberly.

"Well, at first I thought it was just my imagination," Christina said, her voice rising. "Then I thought it was because we haven't been spending much time together. Then I thought it was the stress we've both been under. You know, me trying to get Star back in shape, you trying to get short-listed for the team. Then I thought—" She stopped abruptly, then turned away and muttered, "I don't know what I thought."

"What? Tell me," Parker said softly.

Christina was silent for a moment. She scratched Ozzie under his whiskery chin. "Well, we both love horses, but it doesn't seem like we have anything in common anymore. I mean, our goals are completely different."

"Different and the same," Parker admitted with a sigh. "You going for the Triple Crown and me going for the Olympics basically means we have no time for anything else in our lives." Reaching up, he pulled a burr from Ozzie's long mane. When Christina didn't say anything, he asked, "So where does that leave us?"

She shrugged and remained silent.

Not a good sign, Parker thought. "How about if we go out Sunday afternoon? I'll finish my chores here early. Dinner or a movie. You pick."

"Parker!" a frantic voice rang from the barn. Turning, Parker saw Justin standing in the doorway with a huge hunk of black horsehair in his hand.

56

"Uh-oh. That doesn't look good." He turned back to Christina. "I'd better go help him. So, are we on for Sunday?"

"Okay," Christina said as they started for the barn, but she sounded more hesitant than excited. "*If* we can both find the time."

"Parker, you've got to quiz me on this dressage test," Kaitlin said.

Parker nodded absently. He was pulling gear from his pickup truck, trying to find Foxy's girth. It was Saturday morning, and Parker, Tor, and six Whisperwood students had just arrived at Lexington Farms for the one-day trial.

"I keep forgetting what happens after I change rein at R," Kaitlin continued, her voice rising anxiously.

Where is my girth? Parker fumed. That morning, three students had ridden with him to Lexington Farms. The night before, when the kids had loaded the equipment in his truck, they'd thrown everything in with no rhyme or reason.

"And I can never remember where I'm supposed to circle left—"

"Why don't you ask Alicia or one of the other kids to quiz you?" Parker asked.

"They're all busy doing something important."

Turning, Parker glowered at her. "You mean I'm the only one *not* doing anything important?"

Kaitlin flushed. "I didn't mean it that way. But you're my instructor. You're supposed to help."

Parker raised his eyes to the sky. *I bet Hap Palmer and Mark Donnelly never had to mess with whiny kids.* He'd already spent the morning walking the novice cross-country course with the students. He'd been so busy explaining to them how to handle each obstacle that he'd barely gotten a chance to look at the advanced-level course.

"Listen, Kaitlin," Parker said, trying to stay calm. "This event today is preparation for me and Foxy. It's our last competition before Rolex, and Rolex is my last chance to get noticed by the Olympic selection committee. The *Olympics*," he repeated, emphasizing the name to make sure Kaitlin understood how important it was to him.

Kaitlin heaved a sigh. "You're right. I'll find someone else," she said, but when she trudged off Parker instantly felt guilty.

He was about to call out to her when Foxy whinnied impatiently from the van. Parker clenched his jaw. Why didn't he have a groom like all the other advanced-level riders? Then Foxy could be walking around, stretching her legs and getting used to the sights. But he couldn't afford to pay someone, and none of the students was old enough to handle Foxy. What was he going to do for Rolex? He'd have to have help there.

Christina? Parker quickly dismissed the idea. She'd helped him many times before, but now that Star was healthy, she was far too busy racing him. Kevin McLean had helped Parker at Deer Springs, but now Kevin was immersed in the spring soccer season.

"Just a minute," he called to Foxy before directing his attention back to the truck. *Now, where is that stupid girth?*

Grabbing a tack trunk, he wrestled it off the truck bed, kneeled, and opened it. Just then Samantha drove up with a carload of students who had come to cheer their friends on. Giggling and shrieking, they exploded from the car.

"Hi, Parker!"

"Good luck, Parker!"

"Where's Chili? I have a bag of carrots for him."

"When are you riding, Parker?"

"We'll cheer for you!"

Parker rubbed his temples. *Go away!* he wanted to holler. *Don't cheer for me. Don't talk to me. Just leave me alone.*

"Parker, are you all right?" Samantha asked.

Parker glanced up. Samantha was standing there alone, the kids having scattered as quickly as they'd arrived.

"No, I'm not all right," Parker said, whacking his riding crop against his leg. "Doesn't anyone know how important today is to me? Don't they know I'm an Olympic contender? For just this *one* day it would sure be nice if I didn't have to be an instructor, groom, baby-sitter, cheerleader, and problem solver." He pointed the riding crop at Samantha. "Then I might have a slight chance to win!"

6

SAMANTHA PUSHED THE RIDING CROP AWAY FROM HER FACE. "Parker Townsend, you sound like a spoiled rock star, not an Olympic contender," she told him.

"Hey, Parker, is this your girth?" Parker looked over his shoulder to see Justin pulling Bouncer by the reins and holding out a girth. When they halted, Bouncer's saddle and pad fell to the ground with a thud.

Turning, Parker took the girth. "Yeah, it is."

"Where's *your* girth?" Samantha asked Justin as she picked up the saddle and brushed the dirt off the pommel.

Justin's face turned crimson under his helmet. "I have no idea, and I'm riding my dressage test in fifteen minutes, and Tor says I need to warm up Bouncer and

61

no one's *helping* me!" he wailed, his lower lip quivering.

Oh, no, Parker thought, *that's what* I *sound like.*

"Hey, it'll be okay." Parker patted Justin on the shoulder. "I know just how you feel." He wiped away a tear rolling down Justin's cheek. Competing was hard on everybody. "Don't panic. I think Bouncer's girth is in the tack trunk," Parker said. Kneeling, he rummaged around until he found a short girth. "Here. Let's get the saddle on Bouncer and I'll give you a leg up."

Quickly he and Samantha got Bouncer ready. With a relieved smile, Justin mounted. As Samantha led the pair away, Parker called out, "And remember, Justin— stay relaxed and have fun!"

Justin gave him a thumbs-up. Samantha shot Parker a look that said, *I'll talk to you later.*

Parker blew out his breath. *Crisis averted.* Now he needed to follow his own advice and relax.

Half an hour later he was mounted on Foxy, wearing his black shadbelly coat, high black boots, white gloves, and top hat, ready for dressage. Before he entered the warm-up arena, Samantha came up to him with a clean rag in her hand.

"Was your dressing room satisfactory, sir?" she asked in a prim English accent. "How about the tea? Too hot? Too cold?"

Parker smiled and shook his head. "Okay, Sam, I get your point."

"You'd better have gotten the point. No more tantrums," she said, her tone serious. "And no more barking at the students, correct? Even Olympic contenders have to be nice to little kids who need their help."

Parker raised one hand. "Promise," he said.

Samantha gave his boot a swipe with the rag. "Good. Now go warm up Foxy."

Parker gave her a mock salute. As he trotted Foxy in the warm-up area, she humped her back and swished her tail all the way down one side of the ring. Event horses had to be superfit for the grueling jumping portions, and keeping them calm and responsive for dressage was a major feat. Especially when the horse was as spirited as Foxy.

Sitting deep, Parker forced his whole body to relax. Breathe in, breathe out. His chin bobbed and his body sagged. They trotted in several small circles, changing rein until Parker could feel her grow soft and supple.

Not wanting to overdo the warm-up, Parker slowed Foxy to a walk. Loosening the rein, he let her stretch her neck and walk around the perimeter of the dressage ring while he watched the rider before him finish her test.

He recognized the woman riding a huge Dutch warmblood with beautiful gaits. It was Alyson Findley. She'd won the dressage phase at Thorndale, but her time in cross-country was far too slow.

Thorndale was where I first met Lyssa Hynde, Parker remembered. Lyssa and Soldier Blue had beaten him at Thorndale, and then again at Deer Springs. Now he'd be competing against Lyssa at Rolex. Parker grimaced. Did he really stand a chance against riders such as her?

The bell interrupted his thoughts, and he glanced at the gate. Alyson had ridden from the arena. Parker wished he'd been paying more attention, since Alyson would be one of the riders to beat.

Taking a deep breath, Parker adjusted his top hat and gathered his reins. He had no idea why doubts about Rolex were suddenly cropping up now, but he had better shake them out of his mind. He had three phases of a one-day event to get through, and Foxy deserved his undivided attention.

"Way to go, Parker!"

"Way to go, Justin!" Parker gave Justin a high five, and they slapped palms.

The two were standing in front of the bulletin board where the scores for the different levels were posted. Justin had received a 54.34 percent in the novice division, which was great for his first time. Foxy had scored a 44.67 percent, good enough to put them in fourth place in the advanced division. Since dressage wasn't Foxy's strength, Parker was pleased—especially since the horses who placed first, second, and third were not nearly as strong as Foxy in the jumping phases. Unless something unexpected happened, he'd have little trouble pulling into first place after cross-country.

"Let's go pick up our tests," Parker told Justin.

Justin wrinkled his nose. "Tests? You mean now I have to take a test? But I didn't study!"

Laughing, Parker ruffled Justin's hair as they headed for the secretary's booth. "You already took the test. That's what you and Bouncer did in the arena. The judges wrote remarks and gave you points on a score sheet. That's what we're going to pick up."

When they reached the small building and went inside, Parker stopped short. A man was leaning on the desk counter, talking to one of the officials. It was the U.S. Equestrian Team chef d'equipe, Mark Donnelly. Not only did Parker recognize him from photos, but the man was wearing a cap with the USET logo on it.

What was he doing here?

"May I help you?" a woman behind the counter asked. Parker gave her their numbers, and she went to find their test sheets. While he waited, Parker tried to listen to what Captain Donnelly was saying to the official. They were discussing the cross-country course. Parker knew that none of the horse-and-rider teams competing at Lexington Farms was on the USET's short list. So why was Donnelly hanging around?

"Here you go." The woman slid the tests across the counter. Justin snatched his up. As he read it, his eyes widened. "Wow! The judges gave me lots of sixes and sevens! That's great, right, Parker?"

"Right," Parker murmured, his attention on the comments on his own sheet. *Good forward energy, excellent suspension*—the only negative comment the judges had made was about Foxy's initial resistance with the first flying change.

Parker wasn't worried about that. Foxy had just been reminding him that she was only working hard because she *wanted* to, not because Parker was making her.

What he *was* worried about was Captain Mark Donnelly.

As Parker left the secretary's booth, he glanced over his shoulder. Captain Donnelly was still talking to the official, but his gaze was on Parker. Parker whipped his head around and pushed open the door. Did Donnelly know who he was? Was it possible he was here to watch *him*?

"I'm hungry," Justin said.

"Let's go find your mom and dad," Parker suggested.

Half an hour later Parker was striding back to the

Whisperwood van, which was parked by his pickup truck. Kids, parents, and horses bustled around the vehicles as they prepared for their cross-country rides. Parker was dying to ask Samantha if she knew why Captain Donnelly was there. But Sam was adjusting the Velcro straps on Mary's protective vest and holding Chili so Penny could get the girth tightened. Plus someone's father was complaining to her about his daughter's dressage score.

This definitely wasn't the time to ask her about Captain Donnelly.

"Need help?" Parker asked instead.

"Please help Justin with Bouncer," Samantha said, sounding grateful. "Tor had to warm up Curious, so he's been no help at all."

Parker found Justin, who was trying to coax Bouncer into accepting the bit. But Bouncer had his head in the air, and his ears were pinned stubbornly.

Parker whipped a Polo mint from his pocket. "When in trouble, use bribery," he told Justin, and handed him the mint. Justin held it in his palm. Immediately Bouncer lowered his head, and when he opened his mouth to eat the mint, Justin stuck the bit in his mouth.

"Thanks, Parker," Justin said. "You're the greatest."

Remind me of that when I lose at Rolex, Parker thought.

When all the horses and riders were ready, Parker looked for Samantha. But she was heading off with Penny and Chili, who were going early in the novice cross-country.

He'd have to catch her later. Until then he could only hope that the chef d'equipe was at Lexington Farms to watch him compete.

A whinny rang out from the van. Foxy was in one of the narrow stalls, eating from her hay net. Half her hay was scattered over the floorboards, and she stamped her hoof impatiently.

"Let me get changed first, and then I'll get you out of there," Parker said as he came up the ramp. They weren't going cross-country for another forty-five minutes, but he didn't want her cooped up any longer than necessary. He'd already pulled out her braids and wet her mane, so it was no longer frizzy. Stooping, he unwrapped a protective bandage and felt her leg. It was cool.

He slipped her a Polo mint and then hurried down the ramp. In their haste to get ready, the students had scattered brushes, buckets, drink cups, and clothes everywhere. His truck door hung open. Parker peered inside. The front seat was piled with stuff, and some-one had spilled a soda on the floor.

Working quickly, Parker reorganized what he could, finding his cross-country gear in the process.

All except his yellow short-sleeved shirt, which *should* have been on the hanger. Finally, he found the shirt crumpled under a bucket, a wet stain on the back.

Well, this isn't a fashion show, he told himself. Besides, the protective vest and number pinny would cover the stain. Pulling off his sweatshirt, he slipped the yellow shirt over his head, wincing when the cold, wet spot hit his back. Then he double-checked his stopwatch and slipped on the armband with all his medical information on it. All the advanced riders wore them in case they were severely injured. Now it was time to get Foxy.

Half an hour later they were both ready. By then some of the younger riders were straggling back from their cross-country rides. They were exhausted and muddy. A few had tear streaks on their dirty cheeks.

Penny came up and buried her head under Parker's arm. "Chili stopped on top of the bank and wouldn't go down it."

Parker patted her on top of her helmet. "The bank here probably looked scarier to Chili than the one at Whisperwood. Did it look scarier to you?"

Penny nodded her head. "I was so embarrassed. The fence judge had to lead me around it. I got so many penalty points!"

Parker kneeled so he was at eye level with Penny. Foxy danced beside him, eager to get moving. "Hey, you got around the whole course. That's awesome for your first event! I think you should give Chili one of these." He handed her a Polo mint. "And here's one for you, too!"

Taking the mints, Penny smiled through her tears, then turned to feed one to Chili.

Parker rechecked his gear, making sure Foxy's protective boots were secure, and left before he could run into another student. Halfway to the warm-up area he realized he didn't have his riding gloves with him. Well, he probably wouldn't be able to find them anyway.

"Ready?" Tor asked as he rode up on Curious.

"Almost. Hey, how'd Curious do?" Parker asked.

"Lots of time penalties," Tor said. "We circled a lot so he could get a good look at all the obstacles. I think Penny and Chili even beat me," he added with a chuckle. "When's your ride?"

Parker checked his watch. "One forty-five. Hey, can I borrow your gloves? Mine are lost somewhere in the truck."

"Sure." Tor peeled them off and handed them to Parker. "They're sweaty, so let them dry out a little. And good luck," Tor added as he started to ride off.

"Hey, did you notice that Captain Donnelly was here?" Parker called.

Turning in the saddle, Tor said, "Donnelly?" as if he

wasn't sure whom Parker was referring to. "Uh, yeah, I did see him."

"Did you talk to him?" Parker pressed. "Did he say why he was here?"

Exhaling slowly, Tor looked down at the reins in his hand, as if trying to avoid Parker's eyes. "As a matter of fact, I did talk to him," he said, his tone vague.

"And what did he say?" Parker asked impatiently.

"I can't remember exactly," Tor began, but then he cut his eyes to Parker and said, "All right, I might as well tell you. Donnelly said he was here to watch a horse and rider."

Parker's brows rose under the brim of his helmet. "Who?"

Tor bit back a grin. "I think he mentioned he was watching a horse named Foxglove—and her rider, some guy named Townsend."

Parker's jaw dropped.

"Wait a minute." Tor snapped his fingers, then pointed at Parker. "That's you!"

7

"WHY DIDN'T YOU TELL ME?" PARKER ASKED. "SAM DIDN'T say anything, either."

"Sam didn't know," Tor said. "And I only just talked to Captain Donnelly a minute ago. I wasn't going to tell you until after your cross-country ride. I know how hyper you can get."

"Hyper? Me, hyper?" Parker cracked his knuckles, then paced in front of Foxy, feeling as if he were about to burst. "No, I'm glad you told me. I'll be fine." He spun around. "Did he say *why* he was watching me?"

"All he said was your name has come up a few times as a possible candidate for the short list."

Parker felt a rush of excitement.

"That doesn't mean you should change anything, Parker," Tor warned. "Warm up Foxy and ride the course as if Donnelly weren't here. You know what you need to do for a clear round with no time faults."

Parker cracked his knuckles again, too excited to reply.

"Parker? Did you hear me?"

Parker glanced up at Tor. "I heard you."

"Then snap out of it and get Foxy warmed up," Tor said firmly. "Olympic contenders have to keep their heads on their shoulders."

Parker nodded and led Foxy away as if in a daze. Why was he in such shock? He'd been hoping that someone from the USET or Olympic selection committee would notice him and Foxy. He just hadn't been expecting it to happen that day.

When he reached the warm-up area, Parker pulled down his stirrups and checked his girth. Foxy's ears were rotating wildly, and she pranced at the end of the reins. Cross-country was her favorite phase, which was one reason they did so well in it. Foxy saw each obstacle as a challenge and approached it with all the speed and agility she could muster.

Smiling, Parker patted her silky neck. "It's about time somebody noticed you," he told her, feeling pumped. "Captain Donnelly's eyes are going to pop out of his head when he sees what an awesome jumper you are. He'll put us on the list before we even finish the course!"

Foxy shook her mane as if to say, *Then let's get going*. Parker mounted, barely making it into the saddle before the mare jogged off—right into the path of another horse.

"Sorry, sorry." Parker touched the brim of his helmet, then let Foxy trot at her own speed around the flat area, his reins loose. He could tell by her carriage and gait that she was ready to go, both physically and mentally. Keeping the reins slack, he steered her toward the rail set up in the middle of the schooling area. She approached the fence with a balanced stride, jumped it easily, and landed softly.

Parker patted her fondly on the neck. Foxy was ready to kick butt.

Fifteen minutes later Parker steered Foxy into the starting box. An official with a clipboard stood nearby. Out of the corner of his eye, Parker spotted Donnelly sitting in a golf cart with an event steward, watching.

His pulse quickened.

Seconds later the official began his countdown. "Ten, nine, eight . . ." Parker pushed Donnelly from his mind. ". . . seven, six, five, four, three, two . . ." He wheeled Foxy around. ". . . one . . ." He pressed the stopwatch button on his watch. ". . . zero!" He leaned forward, and Foxy exploded from the box.

She leaped into a reckless gallop, her legs churning, her hooves pounding the hard earth. The first two fences were a hedge and an easy post and rail, and Parker let the mare take them at her own speed. He didn't want to fight with her too early, but when they landed and headed for the third jump, a tricky double bounce, he gathered the reins and settled deeper into the saddle. The course consisted of fifteen obstacles. If he didn't rate her now, she'd burn out before the last jump.

I bet Captain Donnelly's at the bounce, Parker thought. The bounce might not be the biggest fence on the course, but it required a steady and balanced approach, since both fences were set downhill. Riding it well would clearly demonstrate the rider's control.

Thank you, Samantha, for forcing me to work on precision and technique.

Foxy shook her head, fighting Parker's tightened rein. He pushed her forward onto the bit and headed for the first element of the bounce in a collected frame. She jumped it beautifully. Weight on his heels, Parker sat back to help keep Foxy off her forehand down the slope. She took one stride and soared over the second fence.

Atta girl! Parker cheered silently. As Foxy galloped up the hill, he glanced over his shoulder. The golf cart was following him across the field.

If I were Donnelly, I'd head for Lexington Lake. It was a new obstacle, modeled after the Head of the Lake at

Rolex. When Parker had walked the course the day before, he knew it would be the trickiest combination at Lexington. It consisted of three elements—a jump into water, a bank out of the water, then one stride and a second jump. To get through without penalties required a bold horse with tremendous jumping ability.

Foxy was that kind of horse.

Parker took the next five obstacles easily. As they headed for Lexington Lake, which was about halfway through the course, he laid his palm on Foxy's neck. Her skin was warm, not hot, her breathing was rhythmic, and her stride felt strong.

Checking his watch, he knew he was making good time. They didn't have to rush. If they made it through Lexington Lake with no penalties, the rest of the course would be a piece of cake.

They cantered through the woods. Ahead Parker could see a crowd of people flanking the lake. It was definitely the most popular obstacle on the course. As they approached the first element, an angled panel fence, several voices screamed, "Go, Parker!"

Foxy's ears flicked at the noise and the sights.

"This is it, girl," Parker whispered. "The toughest combination. I know you can do it. *We* can do it."

Foxy took the jump boldly. As they sailed over the logs, she cocked her ears, realizing she was sailing through the air toward water. Down, down, down. It

76

seemed as if they were airborne forever. Sitting up, Parker leaned back and let the reins slip through his fingers. Foxy landed with a splash. Water sprayed everywhere, and for a second Parker couldn't see.

The water was over Foxy's knees, and she slowed to a trot. Blinking away the water, Parker took up rein, leaned forward, and squeezed her back into a canter. The jump up the bank took a huge effort, and Foxy would need impulsion to get up it and then over the next fence.

Foxy took the last stride toward the bank, the water dragging at her legs. Parker clamped his own legs against her sides and urged her forward with his voice and body.

She leaped high, scrambled for a hold on the top of the bank, and propelled herself upward. Parker could feel the energy it took, and he tried to help her all he could as she thrust herself onto the bank and toward the next fence.

Steady. One stride. Parker cued her mentally. Foxy pricked her ears and gathered herself before the huge log jump, sailing over it as if it were nothing.

The crowd burst into wild cheers. As they galloped on, Parker praised and patted his incredible horse. Foxy tossed her head as if to say, *You were right—it was easy*.

Seven fences later Parker and Foxy galloped the

last stretch toward the finish. Their time was perfect, and they hadn't received one penalty point.

Foxy galloped past the finish line. Raising one arm, Parker gave out a whoop. Tor, Justin, and Penny were waiting for him with a sweat sheet, a half bucket of warm water spiked with electrolytes, Foxy's halter, and her grooming box.

When Foxy slowed to a walk, Parker jumped off and patted the mare's sweaty neck. Penny and Justin ran up, cheering loudly.

"You were the greatest!" Justin said, giving Parker a high five.

Penny fed Foxy a Polo mint. "I found them in your truck," she admitted.

Tor was smiling. "If anybody beats that round, I'll be surprised. Your time was perfect."

Parker slipped off Foxy's bit, then rubbed her head with a towel. Penny handed him the halter. He buckled it on, swiveling his head to search for Captain Donnelly.

There was no sign of him or the golf cart.

Turning his attention back to Foxy, Parker checked her respiration and heartbeat. She was already cooling down and breathing more regularly.

While Parker was busy with Foxy, Tor held the mare and explained to Justin and Penny what Parker was doing and why.

"Cross-country is very hard on a horse," he said. "If the horse's temperature rises above a hundred and five degrees, you need to call a vet. Sometimes the muscles quiver. That's called the thumps, and it means call a vet, too."

"I'll have to wash down Foxy and walk her for a long time," Parker added. "Until her pulse and respiration are back to normal."

"I had to wash Chili, too," Penny said. "He wasn't as sweaty as Foxy, though."

"Probably because he trotted most of the course," Justin said.

"Bouncer didn't do much better," Penny retorted, defending her mount.

"Did too."

Parker shushed them. "I'm trying to hear Foxy's heartbeat."

When he knew for sure that Foxy was in good shape, Parker again looked around for Captain Donnelly. Penny and Justin wandered off, bored with the routine. Tor stayed to help Parker.

Parker couldn't stand it any longer. "Where's Captain Donnelly? Do you think he saw us? Do you think he'll say anything to me today?"

Tor shook his head. "He left after Lexington Lake."

Parker exhaled with frustration.

Tor clapped him on the shoulder. "Patience. Captain Donnelly doesn't have sole authority to decide who gets on the short list. Sam said that he definitely saw you jump Lexington Lake. And the man had to have been impressed. You were one of the few to make it through with style and pizzazz."

"Pizzazz?" Parker chuckled. "Is that a new eventing term?"

"Must be," Tor said, laughing with him. "'Cause Sam said you and Foxy definitely have it."

Parker shook his head. Again he was disappointed that the chef d'equipe hadn't spoken to him or given him any sign of encouragement.

He tried to shrug it off with a laugh. "Pizzazz, huh? Well, let's just hope Captain Donnelly thought we had it, too."

8

"I CAN'T BELIEVE IT, FOXY," PARKER SAID AS HE RAN HIS hands down the mare's front legs. "No heat. No puffiness. It's hard to believe you just competed in a one-day yesterday and *won*."

It was Sunday morning, the day after Lexington Farms. Parker had arrived early to check on Foxy. After a clean stadium jumping round at the one-day, the pair had won the advanced division.

Parker's only regret was that Captain Donnelly hadn't been there to see him win the trophy.

When Parker straightened, Foxy bumped him with her nose and hung her head over the stall door. "You want out of here, don't you?" Parker said, and snapped a lead line onto her halter. Not that he blamed her. A relaxing day eating and rolling in the mud sounded just right.

He turned Foxy out, watching as she kicked up her heels and then found just the right spot to roll. Since she had the day off, Parker turned his thoughts to Ozzie. If he was going to do something with the big horse, this was the perfect day.

Every Sunday after the morning feeds, Samantha and Tor left to visit family and friends. That meant they wouldn't be there to watch him blunder around with Ozzie.

Carrying the lead line and halter, Parker walked to Ozzie's pasture. "You look like Bigfoot," he said when the big horse ambled over to the gate. His shaggy coat was crusted with mud from ears to tail.

"If you were my horse, I'd give you a bath and a body clip," Parker added as he buckled on the halter. "It'll take forever to groom you."

Parker led Ozzie into the barn, hooked him in crossties, and started currying. Dust and hair flew everywhere. Ozzie stood quietly, head down, eyes half closed, one hind leg cocked. Parker combed out the long mane and tail and picked out the horse's hooves. Finally he stepped back and surveyed his handiwork. The majority of the mud was off, but the horse's coat was still dull with dust.

"Well, that was useless," he muttered. Ozzie

flapped his bottom lip lazily. He looked half asleep.

Grabbing two lead lines, Parker hooked them to opposite sides of the halter. After putting on his helmet, he led Ozzie outside to the mounting block and climbed on. Instantly the horse's head went up, and he strode off eagerly. Startled by the change, Parker had to grab mane to keep from slipping sideways.

He steered Ozzie into the cross-country field. For an hour they walked and trotted up and down hills and through the woods. They leaped over ditches and splashed through streams. Ozzie never hesitated. He responded to the softest tug on the lead ropes and the slightest leg pressure. To halt, all Parker had to do was deepen his seat.

When Parker turned Ozzie back toward the barn, he felt more relaxed than he had in ages. At least for the hour, he'd quit worrying about Captain Donnelly, Rolex, and the short list. He'd even come up with a plan to solve one of his problems. After Kaitlin's lesson on Tuesday, he would ask her to groom for him at Rolex. She was fifteen, an excellent horseperson, and strong enough to handle Foxy. Plus she was a determined competitor. Parker would present Rolex as a learning opportunity for her. And since Kaitlin came from a well-off family, Parker hoped she would groom for free.

As Ozzie strode from the cross-country field,

Parker eyed the jumping ring. The gelding had been such a pussycat on their ride. Should he try taking him in?

Why not? Parker thought. He had to try it sometime. Besides, what was the worst Ozzie could do? Refuse to go in?

Parker grinned cockily. He loved a challenge. Tightening his hold on the lead lines, he steered Ozzie toward the opening into the arena. The horse's ears flicked, but he walked confidently toward the entrance. Parker sat quietly, his long legs hanging loosely, hoping to telegraph confidence.

"Good boy. Just two more steps," Parker said. "Almost there."

Without warning, Ozzie spun clockwise ninety degrees, and Parker flew off in the opposite direction, landing hard on his backside in the soft dirt. Trotting a few feet to a patch of grass, Ozzie dropped his head to graze.

"Ouch," Parker muttered, although his ego was more bruised than his body. He hadn't seen that coming at all.

Propping himself up on one elbow, Parker studied Ozzie. Was he fooling himself to think that he could succeed when Hap Palmer, one of the best jumper riders in the world, had failed?

Still chewing, Ozzie lifted his head and looked

over at Parker as if wondering why he was still sitting on the ground. The horse had such an amiable personality and such great potential that Parker hated to give up. And it *was* his fault he'd gotten dumped. Juanita had warned him about Ozzie's tricks, and he hadn't listened.

So how was he ever going to get Ozzie into the ring?

"Go with what the horse likes," Samantha had advised.

And what did Ozzie like best? Food.

What if he fed Ozzie in the ring? Would the horse learn to associate good things with the ring? The idea sounded like something from the psychology class Parker had taken the previous semester, but he was willing to try anything.

Standing up, he slapped the dirt off his jeans and then caught Ozzie. The big horse followed him obediently into the barn. As soon as Parker opened the door to the feed room, Ozzie whinnied and shook his head.

"You like this stuff, huh?" Parker said as he scooped sweet feed into a bucket. Ozzie shoved Parker's back with his muzzle.

Holding out the bucket, Parker led Ozzie back to the jumping ring, trying to keep the eager horse from trampling him. *So far so good.* But two feet from the opening, Ozzie planted his hooves and stopped dead.

"That's okay. Be stubborn," Parker said as he continued to walk forward. He set the bucket in the middle of the entrance to the ring and pointed at it. "Here's lunch. You don't even have to go into the ring to eat it, just up to the gate. When you get hungry, help yourself."

Ozzie eyed him dubiously. Parker sat down and leaned against the gatepost. When Ozzie tried to move toward the grass, Parker tightened his hold on the lead line. "Oh, no you don't. You just stand there."

Frustrated, Ozzie pawed, bobbed his head, then stretched his neck toward the bucket and wiggled his lips, trying to reach it. But it was too far away.

Parker chuckled. "Smells good, huh?" he said, his own stomach growling. He'd passed up Sunday breakfast at his house, hoping to avoid his parents. He'd have to grab something after Ozzie ate his grain. *If* Ozzie ate his grain, Parker amended. The big horse hadn't budged.

Yawning, Parker rested his head on the post. The sun was warm, and he felt totally relaxed after the ride. He thought about the pile of tack from the day before that needed cleaning and the two yearlings that needed handling, but then his brain grew fuzzy and his eyelids heavy. He tried to keep them open—to watch and make sure Ozzie didn't do something stupid—but they kept drifting shut. Besides, the stubborn horse hadn't moved.

"That's all right, Oz, I've got all day," Parker said, his words slightly slurred. He yawned again, his head lolled sideways, and soon he was dozing.

A horse's snort woke him up. Groggy, Parker rubbed his face with his palm. His neck was stiff and his body ached. He couldn't believe he'd fallen asleep propped up against a fence, holding a horse.

Suddenly Parker recognized the sounds of a horse munching, and his eyes flew open. Ozzie stood right in front of him in the entrance to the jumping ring, his big head shoved into the bucket.

Parker grinned excitedly. Okay, so it wasn't a piaffe or a clear round. But it was a start.

"They're coming tomorrow," Samantha announced late that afternoon as she bustled into the tack room. "That's two days sooner than I thought!"

Parker looked up from the bridle he was cleaning. "Who's coming? Did you and Tor buy a new horse?"

"No, Lyssa and Jeff are coming." Opening a metal supply cabinet, she pulled out two new buckets. "I don't have enough free stalls for their horses, so we'll need to turn out somebody. But who?"

Parker dropped the sponge in the bucket of warm water. After putting Ozzie away, he'd gone to get lunch, then come back to start on the mountain of tack that needed cleaning. He'd been working for over an hour when he'd heard Samantha and Tor come up the drive. Then Samantha had burst into the tack room with her news.

"Why don't you turn out Bentley and Night-hawk?" Parker suggested. "They both love being out. Now that the nights are warmer, they don't need to be cooped up inside."

"Good idea. I'll put Bentley with Ozzie and Tony, and Nighthawk with—" She thought a minute. Nighthawk was a two-year-old Tor had bought at auction. The colt hadn't been gelded or handled much and was still pretty wild.

"Put him out with Chili and Jelly Roll," Parker said. "Those two won't care what kind of stunt he pulls."

Samantha laughed. "Okay. But just for tonight. I don't want the students having to contend with Nighthawk chasing them around the pasture when they have to catch their horses for lessons." She pulled out a bottle of bleach and a large sponge and stuck them in the bucket. "Tonight I want to thoroughly clean their stalls and disinfect them. Do you think you can help me? Tor has a ton of paperwork. We can let them air all night before bedding them. Then tomorrow—" She plucked a piece of paper from her pocket. "I've got a list of things to do before they show up."

Parker chuckled. "You'd think the president was visiting."

"Captain Donnelly's more important than the president," Samantha joked as she stood up with the loaded bucket in her arms. "I want them to be impressed with Whisperwood. We may not have the fanciest eventing barn, but he'll see that it's well organized and that we care about our horses. I learned everything I know from Ashleigh and Mike and how they run Whitebrook."

Parker tensed. Whitebrook. Christina. Their Sunday afternoon date.

He'd forgotten all about it.

He checked his watch. Five o'clock. Was it too late to call? Would Christina realize he'd forgotten?

Parker tossed his cleaning sponge into the sink. "Sorry, Sam. I've got to call Christina."

"Now?" Samantha looked puzzled.

"Something I forgot to do," Parker said, not wanting to elaborate. He hustled into the small office adjacent to the tack room and dialed Whitebrook, hoping no one would answer because he had no idea what to say.

"Christina left already, Parker," Ashleigh said

when she answered. "She went to dinner and the movies with Kevin, Katie, and some other kids. I thought you were going, too."

"I was supposed to meet them but I, uh, got tied up," Parker fibbed. "Where'd they go to eat? Maybe I can catch them there."

"Antonio's Pizza. They left about half an hour ago. I don't know what movie they planned to see, though."

"Thanks, Ashleigh." Slowly Parker returned the receiver to the cradle. What an idiot he was. He was the one who'd made such a big deal about getting together with Christina, then he'd forgotten. He didn't even have a decent excuse.

Would she understand? Or would she tell him to get lost? Well, maybe that would be for the best. Lately he hadn't been much of a boyfriend.

You still have time to meet her at Antonio's, Parker reminded himself.

The thing was, he didn't *want* to meet her. He'd promised to help Samantha. Besides, he didn't have the energy to make up a story or the heart to face Christina's hurt silence.

Face it, Parker Townsend, you're a coward and *a jerk,* a little voice said. *Christina deserves better than you.*

Parker nodded in agreement. He'd call Christina later that night and apologize. And the next time he saw her, they'd have a talk about their relationship—at least what was left of it.

Which isn't much, Parker thought. Sighing tiredly, he stood up and went to help Samantha with the stalls.

Parker leaned on a broom handle and surveyed the spotless barn. It was so clean, it would even pass Samantha's white-glove test.

It was Monday, and Parker had been mucking and raking all morning. Not that he was the only one working. Samantha had been up since dawn, grooming the horses before turning them out. Tor had helped Parker with the stalls, then graded the gravel drive. Now he was touching up the green-and-white Whisperwood sign while Samantha vacuumed the tack room.

Vacuuming the tack room. Parker shook his head. She was going overboard about Captain Donnelly. It was *worse* than a visit from the president.

Parker checked his watch. It was almost eleven. Lyssa and Blue were supposed to arrive at noon. Jeff Steffen and his entourage were coming around one. That gave him an hour to bed their stalls.

The roar of a truck motor made Parker glance out the barn door. A gleaming blue truck pulling a matching four-horse trailer was rolling up the drive.

Nice rig, Parker thought. And brand-new, which

meant it couldn't be Lyssa. Last time she'd arrived at Whisperwood driving a truck and trailer straight out of a junkyard. *Must be Jeff.* Parker set the rake against the wall, eager to meet the famous eventer. He'd read articles about Jeff in magazines and had watched him ride the previous year at Fair Hill, but he'd never met him.

By the time Parker got outside, the driver was circling the truck and trailer around to the entrance of the barn. The slogan Ajax Feed—For the Life of Your Horse was on the driver's-side door. Huffman's Trailers was written in bold letters on the trailer.

Parker made a noise in his throat. *Sponsors. No wonder it's such a nice rig.*

Then the truck stopped, a door slammed, and someone yelled, "Parker!" A second later Lyssa Hynde raced around the back of the trailer.

"I'm so glad to be here!" Throwing herself into his arms, she gave him an exuberant hug. She was dressed in her usual outfit of jeans, cowboy boots, and a western-style shirt in wild colors. Her dark hair fell down her back in a thick braid.

"Lyssa? This is *your* rig?" Parker exclaimed in surprise.

"Yeah. Isn't it a beaut? It even has a dressing area and a tack room"—Lyssa waved one hand at the trailer—"*and* Blue still has two stalls all to himself.

When I loaded him for the trip, he thought he'd died and gone to horsy heaven."

"But how—"

"Ajax Feed!" Lyssa explained with a grin. "They decided the rider they were sponsoring at Rolex shouldn't drive around in a beat-up junker, so they got a local dealer to fix me up."

Wow. Parker whistled under his breath.

The driver's-side door opened, and a lanky guy climbed out. He was about twenty years old and good-looking in a cowboy sort of way.

"Parker, this is Tony Ransom. He's an eventer, too. Offered to be my groom so he could come out here and see what the big fuss is about."

"Hey." Tony settled his cowboy hat on his head, then reached out to shake hands with Parker.

"First time in the East?" Parker asked.

Tony nodded. "Yup. Sure are a lot of buildings and cars. I was glad when we got out here in horse country. It's beautiful."

"Do you train with Lyssa in Montana?" Parker asked.

"Actually, I'm his trainer," Lyssa said. "He's hoping to learn a bit from Captain Donnelly during our sessions."

"That's right. Congratulations on your USET grant," Parker said to Lyssa before turning his attention back to Tony. "Maybe you can ride one of the Nelsons' horses while you're here."

Tony's eyes widened under the brim of his cowboy hat. "That would be great!"

Lyssa gave Tony a playful nudge with her elbow and grinned up at him, a goofy look on her face. "Now, don't be getting too friendly with Parker. He's our competition," she joked.

"I know." Tony grinned down at Lyssa, the same goofy look on his face.

Parker rolled his eyes. Unless he was totally clueless, Tony was more to Lyssa than a student and a groom.

"Are we finally here?" a voice drawled from the other side of the truck.

"We're here, Aunt Gwen," Lyssa called as an older woman came around the front of the truck, holding her hip and walking stiffly.

"Thank goodness," Aunt Gwen grumbled. Like Tony and Lyssa, she was dressed comfortably in baggy jeans and a long-sleeved western-style shirt. "One more mile just might have done me in."

"Parker, meet my aunt. My parents sent her along as my assistant—*and*," Lyssa added in a whisper, holding up her hand to hide her mouth, "my chaperone."

"That's not completely true," Gwen corrected. "I may help you out a bit, but mostly I'm here to visit friends in Louisville. Thought I'd hitch a ride in Lyssa's fancy-shmancy truck."

As the three talked about their arduous drive from Montana, Parker glanced from one to the other. He could hardly believe what he was hearing and seeing. Lyssa had a new truck, new trailer, a groom, a boyfriend, an assistant, a USET grant, and two sponsors.

No wonder Lyssa got picked for the short list and I didn't, Parker thought. She was way ahead of him. If he wanted to get picked, he'd better get going. First place at Lexington Farms wasn't enough. He'd have to do more.

9

"I FINALLY FOUND YOU," PARKER SAID AS HE OPENED STAR'S stall door. It was Tuesday evening, and Parker had stopped at Whitebrook before going to his world history class. Christina was kneeling in the straw, wrapping Star's legs for the night. "Ashleigh told me you were out in the barn."

"Hi. I'll be through here in a minute," Christina said without looking up.

Stepping into the stall, Parker took hold of Star's halter and scratched the Thoroughbred's forehead. He didn't know what to say. He knew he had to apologize to Christina in person for missing their date on Sunday. He also needed to explain how busy he was going to be for the next few weeks. He just didn't know where to start. No matter what he said, he couldn't make things better between them.

Parker ran his palm down Star's neck. The colt's gold-red coat glowed, his muscles rippled, and his eyes gleamed with life. "Star looks amazing. What race is he running next?"

Christina shrugged. "I'm not sure. There's so much hype about the Derby, it's overwhelming."

"Kind of like these weeks before Rolex," Parker said, nervously cracking his knuckles. "You should see Sam. She's been running around cleaning and organizing the barn like a crazy person." When he'd phoned Christina the night before, he'd told her about Lyssa's arrival. "Jeff and his people finally showed up around ten this morning," Parker continued. "It's no wonder he was a day late. He had a whole town with him in his hundred-thousand-dollar horse van. Two perfect horses, a publicist, and two grooms. He even has a vet coming down from Vermont to be on call. And all his equipment is brand-new."

"Sounds like what we see all the time at the track," Christina said as she moved to do another leg.

Parker snorted. "It's no wonder he and Lyssa got picked for the short list. With all those people helping them, all they have to do is ride."

"Jealous, huh?" Christina chided.

"No. I can handle it," Parker said. Then, taking a deep breath, he added, "Chris, I, um, wanted to apologize for Sunday night. I had a ton of tack to clean, and then Sam found out Lyssa and Jeff were coming early, so I—" His voice trailed off. His excuses sounded lame even to him.

"You don't need to apologize," Christina said, her tone cool. Parker moved toward Star's flank, trying to see her face, but Christina stood up abruptly and walked around to Star's other side. "I know you're busy." Kneeling, she started on the other front leg. "I'm just sorry you missed the movie."

"What did you see?"

"Some comedy. It was okay."

"I could have used a good laugh," Parker said under his breath. For a second he racked his brains, trying to figure out how to bring up their relationship. Obviously, Christina knew there were problems, too.

"Listen, Chris, I know that lately we haven't seen much of each other," he said haltingly. "And I'm afraid that it's only going to get worse. Rolex is—"

Standing, Christina raised her hand like a stop sign. "You don't need to explain. I've been just as busy as you. It seems like there's just no time for us. I mean, when's the last time we had a real date?"

"Uh-h-h . . ."

"I didn't think you'd remember," Christina said.

"In two weeks you've got Rolex, and I'll be prepping Star for his next race sometime after that. That means for the next month all we'll be doing is breaking dates, then apologizing to each other. That's not exactly what you'd call having a relationship." Dropping her chin, Christina looked down at the bandage in her hand. "Maybe we should just cool it for a while, to keep either one of us from getting hurt."

Parker's jaw dropped. Christina peeked up at him, tears glimmering in her eyes. "We can still be friends, and when things slow down, we can see how we feel about each other," she said. Turning quickly, she hurried from the stall. Speechless, Parker could only stare after her.

He couldn't believe it. Of course, Christina was only saying what *he* had wanted to say. But Parker hadn't realized he would feel quite so surprised.

Or quite so hurt.

"Think of it as a great advertising opportunity," Parker said to Mr. Harner, the owner of Harner Feeds. "My mare, Foxglove, and I just won the advanced division at Lexington Farms. We're planning on doing just as well at Rolex. When we win the gold, everyone will see Harner Feeds win the gold, too." Parker waved his hand in an arc, as if pointing out a marquee.

Mr. Harner squinted as if trying to picture it, then spat a squirt of tobacco juice on his warehouse floor. "Well, I dunno," he drawled. "I don't go in for all that fancy advertising. Good service, good product, that's what keeps me in business."

Be patient, Parker told himself.

It was Wednesday morning, and Harner Feeds was the fourth business Parker had visited. At the first three he'd had no luck. Either they weren't interested or they were already sponsoring someone else. Parker had started soliciting too late.

Parker took a deep breath. "That's what we can say on your banner—Harner Feeds—Good Service, Good Product. What do you think?"

"Well, it does have a nice ring." Harner rubbed his chin as if thinking about the idea.

Come on, go for it, Parker urged silently. Lyssa's new rig and Jeff's professional entourage of grooms and assistants had convinced him that a sponsor was one way out of his financial nightmare. He only wished he'd gotten one sooner.

"Foxy and I are the only *local* riders," Parker pressed on. "Over fifty percent of the people attending are from Kentucky. Think how proud they'll be to have a Kentucky boy win, and of course I'll mention Harner Feeds every chance I get."

Harner nodded. "Well, maybe you've got a point. Lemme go in my office and write you a check."

When Harner left the warehouse, Parker punched the air with his fist and danced around a stack of feed bags. *Yes! Money!* His Rolex problems were solved. Tuesday after Kaitlin's lesson, he'd asked her about grooming, and she'd been so excited about it, he wondered why he hadn't asked her sooner.

Harner came into the warehouse holding out a check. "Here you go, young man."

Taking it, Parker pumped the feed store owner's hand. "You won't regret this, sir. Foxy and I will make sure your store is well represented."

"I know you will," Harner said matter-of-factly. "I've got a big banner we used at the Pig Festival, and some key chains and refrigerator magnets. You can pick them up anytime."

"Thank you. Thank you!" Beaming, Parker hurried from the warehouse, climbed into the front seat of his truck, and looked at the check.

It was for fifty dollars.

Fifty dollars!

That wouldn't even cover his food.

Parker groaned and let his head fall back onto the seat. He should have been more explicit about what a sponsor donated in return for handing out key chains.

Now it was too late. And he didn't dare tell anyone how much money he'd received in return for displaying a banner from the Pig Festival.

He'd be the laughingstock of Rolex.

Slowly Parker started the truck and drove from the parking lot. *Forget about sponsors*, he told himself. *Concentrate on training Foxy for Rolex*.

The previous day, after three days of light work, the mare had started back into a tough training regimen. And she was taking it all in stride. That was what mattered. That was what Parker needed to focus on if he wanted to beat the competition at Rolex.

As Parker turned into Whisperwood's drive, he spotted two horses and their riders working in the ring. It was Jeff on Incredible, a gorgeous black Thoroughbred, and Lyssa on Blue, her enormous flea-bitten gray. When the truck drew closer, he also noticed a man standing in the ring with them. Tor? Then Parker recognized the cap with the USET insignia on it.

Captain Donnelly had arrived.

Parker's hands tensed on the steering wheel. He had to get Donnelly to see him ride. Parker doubted that the chef d'equipe would be wowed by his rigorous schedule of mucking stalls, chasing stubborn ponies, and teaching kids to post. If Donnelly saw how well Foxy was performing, he couldn't help but be impressed.

He parked his truck and went into the barn. He had several hours before the lesson students would start arriving. He'd worked Foxy already and his chores were finished, so that left Ozzie. Maybe as he rode the big horse he could think up a way to get Donnelly's attention.

Grabbing a lead line, Parker strode out to the pasture. He had only one more week with Ozzie before the horse went back to Sun Hill. So far, Parker was torn about whether to buy him or not. The gelding was gradually eating his way into the jumping ring. As long as his head was in the bucket, he didn't seem to notice that he was moving farther and farther into the hateful ring. And he loved the trails. Parker had galloped him over rough terrain and jumped him over ditches, water, logs, and brush, and so far nothing had fazed him. This afternoon, however, Parker needed to try something new. He wanted to jump him over a typical cross-country fence, one that Ozzie had never seen in his stadium-jumping career.

Parker knew just what fence to try—the zigzag. It was four feet high and constructed of heavy logs in the shape of a lightning bolt, making the takeoff point hard to judge. The way Ozzie reacted to the zigzag would be an important test to see how suitable he'd be for eventing.

Parker brought Ozzie in the barn and groomed

him. As always, Ozzie stood like an old plug, his lower lip hanging while Parker brushed him. But the instant Parker jumped on his back, the big horse strode off at a brisk walk.

When they reached the far gate that led into the cross-country field, Parker started to dismount so he could open it. Then his gaze settled on the log jump built into the fence for the foxhunters. It was only about two and a half feet high.

Why not?

Circling Ozzie at a trot, Parker aimed him at the jump. Without breaking stride, Ozzie popped over it, flicked his tail, and headed down the hill at a canter. Parker leaned forward and urged him into a gallop. The big horse stretched out his neck, his long legs pumping.

Parker's face broke into a grin. He loved Foxy because she was so nimble and fast. But Ozzie was taller than the mare and incredibly powerful, with a ground-eating stride like a racehorse. Parker could feel the horse's muscles churn and hear the steady rhythm of his breathing. Ozzie could probably run all day and never get tired, which meant he'd have no problems making time on a cross-country course.

When they reached the zigzag, Parker collected Ozzie, preparing to jump. His heartbeat quickened. He'd never jumped a fence this size bareback. And he'd never jumped Ozzie over anything this big. Was he asking too much?

He'd soon find out.

Parker aimed Ozzie for the middle point, then sat quietly. He wanted to see what the horse would do without any aids or encouragement. Ozzie's ears flicked, and his head went up. Without hesitating, he leaped over the fence, his front legs tucked against his chest. Parker grabbed mane and tightened his calves against the horse's sides. Up, up, up they soared, as if they were flying. Halfway over, Parker glanced down. They were clearing the top log by a foot.

They landed smoothly. *All right!* Parker silently cheered. Ducking his head, Ozzie pulled the lead-line reins from Parker's grasp, humped his back, and threw out his hind legs in a mighty buck.

Parker shot over Ozzie's head and somersaulted across the grass. He landed flat on his back, staring skyward. Catching his breath, he mentally surveyed his body parts. Nothing hurt. He moved each arm and leg. Everything worked.

A snort made him roll his eyes backward. Ozzie was standing behind his head. All Parker could see was the horse's muzzle as he lipped at his helmet.

Reaching up, Parker scratched the big horse affectionately under his chin. "Ozzie, you big lug, you flew over that zigzag like it wasn't even there." Sitting up, he faced the big horse. "Do you know what that means?"

It means that I want this horse, Parker suddenly realized. But then a darker thought filled his head. Clowning around bareback on the cross-country course was one thing, but would he ever get Ozzie over his problems so that they could actually compete?

Parker frowned with indecision. He was already plagued with worries about Rolex and getting on the team. And he had no money. He couldn't afford a mistake.

Which meant it was just too risky to buy Ozzie. Sighing, Parker rubbed the horse's furry cheek, wishing things were different.

But unless things changed drastically in the next week, he'd have to send Ozzie back.

10

OUT OF THE WOODS CAME THE SOUND OF SOMEONE CLAP-ping. Lyssa was riding toward Parker on Blue. All week she'd been riding in western gear, but now she was dressed in breeches, black boots, and a black velvet helmet. The only western touch was her silver belt buckle.

"That was a fine jump," Lyssa said with a laugh, "but your dismount was a little rough."

Parker grinned. "I haven't had as much experience riding bareback as you have." Rising to his feet, he brushed himself off. "I almost didn't recognize you without your turquoise chaps. But I hear Captain Donnelly is a stickler for good turnout."

"Your horse jumped that zigzag with a foot to spare," Lyssa said, ignoring Parker's comments. She eyed Ozzie appreciatively. "He reminds me of old Blue here. They're not much in the looks department, but they can jump anything."

Parker reached up and ruffled Ozzie's mane. "Did Sam tell you about his problems?"

She nodded. "She also said you've been doing well with him. Do you think you'll buy him?"

"I'd love to. He's awesome. Sound, sane—well, almost sane—athletic, powerful . . ."

"Then go for it," Lyssa said.

Parker shook his head. "I can't. It's too risky. I'll have to take out a bank loan to buy him, which means if he doesn't pan out, I'll be in big trouble. And I'm already in debt."

"I know the feeling," Lyssa said. "Thank goodness for sponsors. But Parker, any horse you buy will be a gamble. They all have quirks and problems. Just ask Jeff Steffen. The first year he had Incredible, the horse bucked him off every time he got on him. You've been lucky with Foxy. Even Blue took time. He was such a klutz as a three-year-old that he fell whenever we tried to canter. And you should hear some of the stories Captain Donnelly tells about the 2000 Olympics. Some of the horses were total prima donnas."

For a second Parker didn't respond. Then he rubbed his jaw and said, "And here I'd just finished convincing myself that I shouldn't buy him."

Lyssa's brows rose under her helmet. "You mean you're actually listening to me? That's a change," she added teasingly.

Parker chuckled. The last time they'd seen each other, Parker had had a hard time stomaching Lyssa's advice. He was too plain stubborn.

"If I *did* buy him," Parker continued, "how would I get rid of his problems?"

Lyssa thought a minute, her fingers playing with Blue's mane. "If he was my horse, I'd start him with round pen training. Begin at the beginning—you know, gaining his trust on the ground."

Parker draped one arm over Ozzie's withers and listened intently.

"When he was ready to accept tack, I'd throw on a hackamore and western saddle. He certainly isn't going to associate those with his jumping career. At the same time, keep feeding him in the ring. While he's eating, gradually make him do things like move away from the bucket, wait for a minute before he eats, groom him, pick up his feet—that kind of stuff. Then one day, when he's calm, I'd jump on him while he's eating."

Parker crooked one brow. Lyssa made it all seem so sensible and simple.

"It may take a while," Lyssa added seriously. "And there are no guarantees. What *you* have to decide is if he's worth it."

Slowly Parker slanted a grin at her. "Oh, he's definitely worth it. Thanks. I've been trying to find a reason to buy this horse."

She smiled back at him. "My guess is you won't regret it."

"Lyssa?" Parker could hear Tony calling from the barn.

Looking over her shoulder, Lyssa waved at Tony, then turned back to Parker. "We're going to watch a video of last year's Rolex. Want to come? I'd like to introduce you to Captain Donnelly."

"Sure. I'll follow you back." As Parker set off with Ozzie his legs felt stiff and achy. Gritting his teeth, he tried not to limp. "And Lyssa, don't mention me getting dumped, okay?"

"Okay," she agreed, laughing.

Twenty minutes later Parker headed up to the Nelsons' house, ready to meet Captain Donnelly. His palms were sweaty and his mouth dry. *I feel like some teenager meeting a rock star,* he thought ruefully.

Stomping into the mud room, he took off his boots, then followed the sounds of voices to the family room. Tony, Jeff, Lyssa, Samantha, and Captain Donnelly were all sitting around the TV watching the dressage tests from the previous year's Rolex.

For a second Parker stood in the doorway, feeling awkward. Tony and Lyssa sat close together at one end

110

of the sofa. At the other end Captain Donnelly was talking to Jeff Steffen, a tall, lean guy in his twenties with jet-black hair. Jeff was gesturing toward the TV screen, so Parker knew they were discussing the video.

"Hey, Parker." Samantha stood up. "This is Mark Donnelly. Mark, this is Parker Townsend."

Standing, Donnelly shook hands with Parker. He was shorter than Parker but built like a barrel, with a wide chest and strong arms. Bristly gray eyebrows and deep frown lines added to his formidable appearance.

"Nice meeting you, son," Captain Donnelly said, but he quickly turned his attention back to the screen.

Tongue-tied, Parker could only nod as Captain Donnelly resumed his commentary on the dressage tests. Parker found a seat on the floor by Samantha's feet.

Well, I sure impressed him, he thought wryly. The video switched from dressage to cross-country. For half an hour Parker listened intently as Captain Donnelly and Jeff discussed the various obstacles. The previous year Jeff had competed at Rolex in the three-star event. Captain Donnelly was the only one who had been at the four-star event, assisting several of the USET riders.

"Here comes the Serpent," Captain Donnelly said as a horse and rider approached a zigzag made of logs. "It's very deceptive because there's no ground line."

111

Leaning forward, he tapped the screen where the logs met the ground. "Almost every horse misjudged the takeoff point."

Parker grimaced as the horse in the video took off a stride too soon. His front knees caught the top log, and horse and rider flipped over. Both landed in a heap, but the horse scrambled to its feet and the rider jumped up to grab the reins.

"That was Marion Skeen and Topnotch Girl," Captain Donnelly continued. "Fortunately, they were all right. But the mare was too sore to compete in stadium jumping."

They watched another horse and rider approach the fence. At the last minute they added a stride, and the horse popped straight up into the air, barely making it over the fence.

"So, Townsend, how would you take that fence?"

Startled, Parker stared at Captain Donnelly, realizing the man was talking to him.

"Uh, n-no problem, sir," he stammered. "Foxy can jump anything, and she always lands on her feet."

Captain Donnelly raised one bushy eyebrow. "Nice to have such confidence in your mount," he said. "However, it's also rather foolhardy. Every rider should be prepared to help his horse in case it gets into trouble."

Parker flushed. Captain Donnelly turned away,

directing the same question to Jeff. Parker didn't hear the other rider's response. The blood was rushing too loudly in his ears.

Way to go, Townsend. First time you meet the guy, and you blow it by acting like a cocky know-it-all. Not exactly the fastest route to the short list.

When the video was over, Parker stood up and approached Captain Donnelly. "Excuse me, Mr. Donnelly," he said. "But while you're at Whisperwood, I was wondering if I could watch you teach one of Jeff and Lyssa's lessons."

Tilting his chin up, Captain Donnelly studied Parker. "I can do better than that," he said finally. "Why don't you ride with us tomorrow morning? Nine o'clock sharp."

"Yes, sir!" Parker exclaimed. "Thank you."

Turning, he marched out the family room door before he could say anything stupid. When he reached the kitchen, he drummed his palms against the countertop. He was finally going to show the chef d'equipe what he and Foxy could do.

"Mr. Townsend, bring your horse over," Captain Donnelly called gruffly to Parker, who had just finished warming up Foxy over a simple line of fences.

It was Thursday morning, and Jeff, Lyssa, and

Parker were having their lesson. Mounted on their horses, Lyssa and Jeff waited for their turn outside the gate. Samantha was in the middle of the ring with Captain Donnelly, watching silently and ready to help adjust the fences.

Parker was nervous about impressing Captain Donnelly, and Foxy had picked up on it. She'd jumped the last two fences in such a blur of speed that Parker was embarrassed. Slowing Foxy to a walk, he patted her neck. "It's okay, girl," he muttered under his breath. "I'm nervous enough for both of us."

They halted in front of Captain Donnelly, who was shaking his head. "I know from watching you at Lexington Farms that the two of you have talent," he said, an unmistakable look of disappointment in his eyes. "But talent alone won't cut it at Rolex."

Parker nodded, but at the same time he couldn't help but bristle. The man had only watched them jump two fences, and Parker was understandably nervous. How could he judge them so quickly?

"Rolex will be the most grueling competition you have ever ridden," Donnelly went on. "In order to survive, you and your horse have to be in harmony. That means putting all the pieces together *now* to ensure a perfect jump—balance, control, responsiveness, rhythm, patience, and pace. You can't be fighting your horse during cross-country, or Foxy will be too tired and stiff for stadium jumping."

Parker's cheeks grew hot. *The man must think I'm a beginner!* He glanced at Sam, wondering why she didn't speak up and say how much they'd worked on all those things in their lessons.

"Today you three will jump a small course designed to make you and your horse work together. First, you'll make a series of U-shaped turns over two oxers," Donnelly explained, speaking loudly enough so that Jeff and Lyssa could hear his remarks. He pointed to two fences he'd set up at oblique angles to each other in the middle of the ring. "Second, you'll jump three fences in a serpentine line." He gestured to the far side of the arena. "We'll do them all at three foot six. Then I'll raise them. Try for perfection the first time—clean flying changes, supportive balancing reins, and a straight track in your approach."

Donnelly turned his gaze to Parker. "Don't try for the bold, impressive jump," he continued, his words obviously directed at Parker. "Try for the soft, relaxed jump. You go first, Townsend."

Parker nodded and squeezed Foxy into a canter. His blood was still boiling. The man was treating him like a novice. And he'd always encouraged Foxy's daring jumping style. She hadn't refused an obstacle since he'd owned her. Why should he change things now?

But if he didn't steady his nerves, he and Foxy would completely blow it.

Parker took deep breaths and cantered Foxy in a small circle until she was moving in a smooth, rocking rhythm. Then he aimed her toward the first oxer. Foxy took it easily. Parker rebalanced her and made a sharp U-turn to jump the second oxer. Halfway there Foxy rooted her head as if to say, *This pace is for babies*, but Parker refused to let her go. He sat deeper, his eyes on the next oxer, and she cleared it smoothly.

"Again! Softer this time!" Captain Donnelly hollered.

Parker gritted his teeth. He could feel Lyssa's and Samantha's eyes on him. And was that a smirk on Jeff's face?

I'll show Donnelly this time. I'll show all of them. Making a flying change, Foxy cantered over the two jumps again. Then Parker steered her toward the line of three jumps, set up in an S. Foxy's ears pricked and her head went up, and he could feel her wanting to rush. *He* wanted to rush.

Taking another deep breath, Parker forced himself to think slow and easy. But Foxy wasn't interested in slow and easy. She leaped the first fence with two feet to spare and landed long, so their turn to the second fence was wide and they jumped it too far to the left.

Parker grimaced. That kind of mistake could cost him a knockdown in stadium jumping or a fall on the cross-country course. Quickly he deepened his weight and used his reins to make sure Foxy took the third jump perfectly.

When he slowed to a trot, Captain Donnelly beckoned him over. His arms were crossed in front of his chest.

"I know," Parker said. Pulling off his helmet, he wiped the sweat off his brow. "We rushed the second fence."

"Then this time your round will be perfect," Captain Donnelly stated before going to help Samantha, who was raising the rails.

Parker walked Foxy in a circle until her breathing slowed. He wished he could start all over again.

When the jumps were higher, Parker secured his helmet. *Last chance*, he thought.

This time when Foxy jumped the small course, she was focused and settled, and when they sailed smoothly over the last fence of the serpentine, Lyssa and Samantha clapped.

Captain Donnelly only nodded. "All right. Lyssa, warm up Blue. Townsend, you can take Foxy in and cool her off. Then you should come back and watch Jeff."

"Okay," Parker mumbled. Dismounting, he led Foxy from the ring.

"Parker?" Sam called, and hurried after him. Halting, Parker waited for her. The last thing he wanted now was a lecture from Samantha.

"You may think Donnelly's being hard on you, but I have to agree with him. You can't rush through the course at Rolex. Foxy has incredible scope, but she's going to be tired after cross-country. If you don't use technique and patience, she'll burn out before you even get to stadium jumping."

Except she didn't burn out at Deer Springs and that was a three-day, Parker wanted to remind her. But he really didn't feel like arguing. He was too upset.

"You're right," Parker said hollowly. "Donnelly knows best. I'll try harder next time."

If there is a next time, Parker thought as he led Foxy into the barn. Taking a lesson with Jeff and Lyssa had been stupid. Donnelly *didn't* know best. He didn't know Foxy. Foxy liked taking her fences fast, but when Parker asked her to listen, she did. They were a *team*.

Captain Donnelly might be the best trainer in the world, but Parker knew Foxy better than *anyone*. And he'd prove it by winning at Rolex.

11

"Is this what you really want to do?" Samantha asked as Parker drove to Sun Hill Farms a week later.

Parker nodded. He was gripping the steering wheel so tightly, his knuckles were white.

"You're not going to blame me? Say I talked you into buying him?" Samantha went on.

Parker shook his head.

"You won't be disappointed if Ozzie—"

"Sam," Parker cut her off, "you're driving me crazy. I took out the loan. I've got the check. I'm handing it to Hap Palmer and leaving with no regrets."

"All right. Sorry," Samantha admitted. "It's just that I know Ozzie has been giving you trouble."

"Okay, so Ozzie hates the round pen." Parker turned into Sun Hill's driveway. "But I've only tried

119

him in it twice. With Rolex starting in less than a week, I've barely had any time for him. Weren't you the one who said I needed to learn everything I can from Donnelly and focus on Rolex?"

"I did. And it seems to have done some good." Samantha angled her chin to look at him. "By the way, I haven't seen that chip on your shoulder in a while."

Parker shrugged as he stopped the truck in front of Hap Palmer's office. He had gotten over his initial anger with Captain Donnelly, and whenever he could, he hung around Jeff, Lyssa, and the chef d'equipe, absorbing anything that might help him win at Rolex.

"Donnelly's a good teacher," was all he said.

"And I bet you've learned a lot," Samantha said. "Even *I've* learned a lot."

Parker opened the truck door. Actually, nothing Donnelly had said had been all that life-changing. "Yeah, I've learned a lot. Now let's not keep Palmer waiting."

Samantha put her hand on his arm. "Just one more thing. I know you're disappointed that Captain Donnelly hasn't put you on the short list," she said. "But Parker, you're still young, and—"

Parker put his hand up to stop her. "I know, I know. You don't have to keep reminding me. Listen, I don't want Hap Palmer charging interest because we're late."

Hap Palmer was waiting for them in the office. Pulling his wallet from his back pocket, Parker opened it and took out the check. Eight thousand dollars. Cheap for the Wizard of Oz. Expensive if Ozzie never got over his problems.

Parker swallowed hard. He'd be paying off the bank loan for a few years. It was one more financial obligation he couldn't afford. He'd never admit it to anyone, but he was worried to death about the responsibility.

But he had made his decision. He wanted Ozzie.

"Here you are, Mr. Palmer." Parker handed him the check.

The man didn't even glance at it. Instead he pointed to a form on the desk. "Before I give you Wizard's registration, health forms, and so on, I want you to sign this contract my lawyer drew up. It says that you will not hold me responsible for any problems you have with the horse."

Parker glanced at Samantha, wondering if the form was legal. She shrugged. Picking it up, they read it together.

It was similar to the form Parker had signed when they'd taken Ozzie on trial. It stated that Parker had been informed of Ozzie's problems, which it listed in detail, and that he would not hold Sun Hill or Hap Palmer liable for anything the horse did.

The way it was worded made Ozzie sound like a monster.

Parker clenched his jaw. No wonder Hap Palmer, with all his expertise, had never been able to get anywhere with Ozzie. Without talking it over with Samantha, Parker signed the form.

"Thank you," Parker said. He shook hands with the man, took all the papers, and then left the office with Samantha. When they got outside, Parker looked around at the pristine farm.

"You know, just like Townsend Acres, this place has *everything* money can buy," Parker said. "But just like my parents' place, Sun Hill is missing one crucial thing."

"What's that?" Samantha asked as she opened the truck door.

"Heart," Parker replied. "Something that Whisperwood has loads of." He looked down at the papers in his hand, a smile creeping across his face.

Ozzie would never come back to Sun Hill again—the big horse was his!

"Shadbelly coat, top hat, white breeches, white shirt with stock and pin," Kaitlin read from the list in her hand.

Parker held up two hangers covered with clear

122

plastic. "All here." He hung the hangers on a bridle hook, then turned back to the pile of equipment spread across the tack room floor. It was Monday, the day before they would leave for Rolex, and Parker and Kaitlin were going through the equipment and supplies they'd need for the six days.

The night before, Kaitlin had suggested that they separate and pack the equipment and tack according to what was needed for each phase. Parker had always made lists—it was the only way to keep track of all the gear—but then he'd throw everything haphazardly in his pickup truck. Kaitlin's method made more sense, and he was happy to let her take charge.

That morning Parker and Tor had taken hay, grain, and bedding for Foxy, Blue, and Jeff's two horses over to the barn on the Kentucky Horse Park grounds. Since the horses would be stabled at the grounds from Tuesday through Sunday, they needed a lot of supplies.

The next morning Parker would take the rest of the gear and unload it at the barn. The horses would arrive Tuesday afternoon. Foxy was getting a ride with Blue in Lyssa's new trailer.

"Wait, I almost forgot white gloves. Add these to the dressage pile, too," Kaitlin said, handing him a brand-new pair.

Taking them, Parker glanced up at her. "These aren't mine."

Kaitlin rolled her eyes. "Yours were too dirty, even after bleaching them, so I bought you new ones. They're a good-luck present."

"Thanks." Parker grinned as he put them with the rest of his dressage clothes. "You know, I owe you a couple of free lessons for all you've done this past week."

"You can repay me by kicking butt so I can point and say, 'That dude is my trainer!'" Kaitlin said before turning back to the task. "Okay, now let's make sure we have all of Foxy's dressage tack—saddle, girth, breastplate, and pad." She touched everything as she named it. "All clean and oiled, by the way."

"You didn't have to do that, Kaitlin," Parker protested. "I was going to get to it, uh, tonight."

"When? After midnight?" Kaitlin asked. "You've been running around like a nutcase as it is. Besides, isn't that part of the groom's job?"

"Actually, no," Parker said. Lowering his voice, he added, "Jeff has a separate guy to take care of his equipment. All his groom does is pamper those two horses. They're cleaner than I am."

Kaitlin laughed. "You want me to spoil Foxy like that?"

Parker shook his head. "No way. She loves her roll in the dirt after her workouts."

"Speaking of dirt, let's put everything in these protective bags." Kaitlin held up several green nylon bags with a white stripe. "After all that saddle-soaping and polishing, I don't want a speck of dust on this stuff."

"Good idea, but where'd you get those?" Parker asked.

"Sam loaned me hers. Yours were too yucky."

"Yucky?"

"Parker, you're riding at Rolex," Kaitlin declared as she slid the bridle into one of the bags and zipped it up. "It's a big deal. Thousands of people will be there. Do you want to look good or what?"

"Okay, okay. You don't have to tell me what a big deal it is," Parker said.

"What happened in here?" Samantha asked as she came into the tack room from the office. "Having a yard sale?"

"We're packing for tomorrow," Kaitlin explained.

Samantha glanced at the neat piles. "This can't be Parker's stuff. Usually his is in one tangled heap in the back of his truck."

"Kaitlin says I have to get organized or she'll refuse to be seen with me at Rolex," Parker joked.

"Well, I'm glad to see someone's keeping you in order." Samantha extended her hand, which held four tickets. "Here, these came for you. They're for tomorrow night."

Parker took them and read out loud, "'The mayor

requests your presence—'" Without finishing, he thrust them at her. "These can't be for me, and even if they are, I'm not going."

Samantha shoved them right back. "They were addressed to you, and you *are* going. This is the introductory dinner, where all the Lexington bigwigs gather at Rolex to meet the competitors."

"You mean they gather to meet riders like Jeff and Dave Breen," Parker corrected. "Riders who are already on the short list. I'm a nobody."

"You won't be a nobody if you introduce yourself," Samantha argued.

"Yeah," Kaitlin chimed in. "You might even get to schmooze with some potential sponsors. You know, Parker, next time I might not groom for free," she added teasingly.

Parker stared at the tickets. "Oh, all right," he finally grumbled.

"Yes!" Kaitlin and Samantha slapped palms

Parker eyed them suspiciously. "Wait a minute. What's going on?"

"There are four tickets, dummy." Samantha fanned them out. "One for you, one for me, one for Tor—"

"And one for me!" Kaitlin exclaimed as she plucked a ticket from Samantha's hand.

Parker rolled his eyes. "So wanting me to go had

nothing to do with my Olympic dreams. You guys just wanted to go to the party."

Laughing, Samantha said, "It was a *little* bit about your future," she admitted. "But yeah, it sounds like a cool party."

When Samantha left, Parker and Kaitlin continued to work. Finally Kaitlin announced, "Done!" after shoving the last bag in the passenger side of Parker's truck.

"Good. It's almost time for my lessons," Parker said as he shut the truck door.

Kaitlin's mouth fell open. "You're teaching lessons? The night before the biggest event of your life?"

"Why not?" Parker asked.

Kaitlin shook her head in disbelief, and Parker shrugged. Just because the next day was the start of the most important six days of his life didn't mean he could drop everything else he had to do.

Grinning, Parker thanked Kaitlin, then headed into the barn to get the lesson horses ready. For the first time, he felt confident about Rolex. He didn't need Captain Donnelly, big-name sponsors, a fancy rig, or his own vet.

He had a great groom, a great trainer, a fantastic horse, and a positive attitude—it was a winning combination. It had to be.

• • •

"What do you think of your fancy digs, Foxglove?" Parker asked as he led the mare inside her spacious stall. It was Tuesday afternoon, and they had finally arrived at the Kentucky Horse Park.

Parker unsnapped the lead and stepped back. Ears pricked, Foxy snorted at the newly laid straw and then sniffed the water bucket, which Parker had brought from home. "I put in extra straw and the finest hay."

Foxy whinnied at Incredible, Jeff's horse, who was stabled to her left. He pressed his nose against the bars between their stalls, and Foxy squealed. On their right, Lyssa was getting Blue settled.

Parker gave Foxy one last pat before heading out to get the rest of the supplies from his truck. As he secured the stall guard, he grimaced at the gaudy Harner Feeds banner that Kaitlin had draped across the front of the stall. A bright red bucket filled with key chains and refrigerator magnets was under the sign. Parker was amazed to see that half of them were already gone.

Sticking his hands in his pants pockets, he wandered down the barn aisle. As he looked at the horses in their stalls, he felt a rush of excitement. Riders from seven different countries were competing at Rolex, and their horses were all stabled together. Grooms chatted to each other in different languages. Several times Parker stopped in front of a stall door to ogle a famous horse he'd seen in a magazine photo.

That was when it hit him. This wasn't Lexington Farms or Deer Springs. He was at Rolex, competing against riders who'd been winning at four-star international events for years. The odds of beating them were about a million to one.

Had he been fooling himself all this time?

The next morning was the briefing of the competitors, then the official course walk. He and Samantha planned to walk the cross-country course as many times as it took to come up with a surefire strategy for getting around with no penalties. Then, at three o'clock, the horses would be inspected. Foxy would have no problem passing the vet check, he was sure of it. The only thing he was worried about was himself.

Quit worrying, Parker scolded himself as he strode from the barn to his truck. *Great groom, great trainer, fantastic horse, and a positive attitude, remember?*

That night Parker stopped by Foxy's stall on the way to the introductory dinner. She stuck her head over the stall guard, and he scratched her chin, trying not to get too much hair on his light blue shirt and khaki pants. Since he was commuting to the Kentucky Horse Park to save money, he had gone home to change after getting her settled.

"I see you've got water, hay, and good company," Parker said, nodding at Incredible, who was watching him through the bars. "I'll check on you before I go home."

Leaving the barn, Parker made his way to the big tent, which pulsated with the sounds of music and laughter. A man dressed in livery checked his ticket, then ushered him inside. The place was packed. A jazz band played on a temporary stage constructed at the far end. In front of the stage, a crowd danced to the music. Tables for dining surrounded the dance floor.

Parker sauntered over to the food table. An ice sculpture of a jumping horse sat in the middle of the trays of canapés, shrimp, crab balls, and dips. As he piled food on his plate, he hunted for Tor and Samantha. Lyssa and Tony waved from the crowd, where they were dancing. Both were dressed in western wear, but neither seemed to care that the band wasn't playing country music.

Parker waved back, then picked up a sandwich cut in the shape of a horseshoe. It reminded him of something his mother would have the cook make for one of her many parties.

Just then a woman's voice rang out over the noise.

"Oh, at Townsend Acres our horses are each assigned a groom. We treat them like our children."

Parker froze, the horseshoe sandwich halfway to his mouth. Was that his *mother?* Parked turned to look, and there she was, Lavinia Townsend, dressed to impress in a gold silk sheath.

Parker's brows shot up in surprise. If his mother was there, so was his father. Parker searched the crowd, and sure enough, he spotted Brad in his trademark gold-buttoned suit coat, talking to a group of well-dressed men.

Parker bit off a hunk of sandwich. His parents had never shown the slightest interest in eventing. All they needed was an invitation from the mayor.

"Parker, darling!" his mother called when she saw him. She flapped her wrist, which sparkled with a diamond bracelet. The sandwich lodged in Parker's throat.

Stay cool, he told himself.

"Mother," Parker said as he approached her, the crowd parting to let him through. "Were you waving at me or showing off your beautiful diamonds?"

"Oh, Parker." Lavinia laughed. "You are such a tease. Come, let me introduce you to Mr. and Mrs. Elsworth." Linking her arm with his, Lavinia dragged him around for the next ten minutes. Anyone watching would have thought they were a loving mother and son. Only Parker noticed that his mother couldn't remember the name of his horse, calling her Foxtail, much less explain what he was doing at Rolex.

"Parker!" A solid clap on the back told him that his father had found them. "If I knew that Binky Davis and Chick Frye were in on this eventing business, I would have gotten interested in the sport sooner."

"So you could convince them to buy a million-dollar Thoroughbred from you and get into racing?" Parker guessed.

Brad pointed a finger at Parker. "Sharp, very sharp. Too sharp to waste your life on this sport. Though I do hear the winner gets a Rolex watch," he added with a sardonic grin.

"Oh, Brad, be nice to your son," Lavinia scolded. "He's got a big day tomorrow. All that jumping."

"No jumping tomorrow, Mother. The jumping phase isn't until—"

"Oh, there's Gloria and Gil Meadows," his mother interrupted. "Brad, we must say hello to them. I haven't seen them in ages."

Excusing himself, Parker left to find Samantha and Tor. After being with his parents, he needed a dose of normalcy.

He finally spotted them talking to several people who wore miniature Irish flags pinned to their lapels.

Since Tor and Samantha had lived in Ireland for years, Parker knew they'd be discussing all things Irish for the rest of the night.

"Parker!" Kaitlin came hurrying over, a glossy event schedule clutched in her hand. "You wouldn't believe all the autographs I've gotten." She flipped the book open and paged through. "David and Karen O'Connor, Blythe Tait, and Abigail Lufkin. Isn't that the coolest?"

"The coolest. You want me to autograph it, too?"

Kaitlin burst out laughing. "No, silly, I'm your *groom*." Suddenly she gasped. "Look, is that Michael Todd? I thought he was retiring. Oh, I have to get his autograph!"

She dashed off, and Parker exhaled loudly. Grabbing a cup of punch, he continued through the noisy crowd. When he spotted Jeff Steffen and Captain Donnelly sitting at a table with plates of food in front of them, he headed in their direction.

He was about ten feet from the table, coming up behind them, when Donnelly leaned toward Jeff and asked, "So what do you think of the Townsend kid?"

Parker stopped in his tracks. Jeff said something, but all Parker heard was ". . . older and more experienced."

Okay, that was understandable. Samantha had said the same thing.

But then Jeff paused, took a sip of his drink, and added in a clear voice, "But that horse of his, Foxglove, is incredibly talented. If the USET would help me raise the money, I'd buy her in a heartbeat and start getting her ready for the Olympics."

Parker wasn't sure he'd heard right. Jeff Steffen and Mark Donnelly didn't think he was ready for the short list, but they wanted *Foxy?*

Well, they aren't getting her, Parker thought angrily. He wouldn't sell Foxy in a million years for a million dollars. He might not be as famous as Jeff Steffen or have as much experience, but he was the best rider for Foxy. And he was going to prove it by beating Jeff and all the others.

Turning, Parker pushed his way through the dancers and headed out of the tent. He wasn't thinking about the Olympic short list anymore. He was going to show everyone. He would win at Rolex—no matter the odds.

12

WEDNESDAY AFTERNOON PARKER SAT IN THE MIDDLE OF the Head of the Lake, the most strenuous obstacle on the course. He'd rolled up the legs of his pants and waded through the thigh-deep water to reach the island, where the second element of the jump was. From his perch on the birch rails, Parker could see the complex obstacle in its entirety.

He stared at it in amazement. In the Rolex video, he'd watched horse after horse jump the Head of the Lake. Some refused. Several fell. But seeing it on TV hadn't prepared him for the size and scope of it.

First, the horse and rider had to jump a ditch and a Normandy bank, which dropped six feet into the lake. They waded through the lake, jumped up a bank onto the island, took two or three strides, and jumped over the birch rails, which again dropped into water. Again, they galloped through water, which was very tiring, leaped up a bank, took one stride, and finished with a jump over a big oxer, the final element.

And after the Head of the Lake there were still ten more obstacles to go.

That morning Samantha and Parker had walked the course with the other American riders, some of whom were competing as a team and some of whom, like Parker, were riding as individuals. At least a dozen of them had competed at Rolex before, so Parker listened to their tales of mistakes—always caused by the rider—and their triumphs, which they usually attributed to their horse's talent or luck.

As he glanced from the Normandy bank to the oxer, Parker shaded his eyes from the sun. He wished he'd worn a cap. The day was unusually warm, and the sun beat down on his head. Already his rolled-up pants legs were drying.

He checked his watch. It was one o'clock. He had two hours before the vet check. Kaitlin was walking Foxy and letting her stretch and graze, so Parker didn't have to hurry. Still, he wanted to have time to finish walking the course.

He jumped off the bank into the water, which felt refreshingly cool. He waded out of the water and up the steep grassy bank, then walked another quarter mile to the Serpent, his wet sneakers rubbing his heels with each step.

"Hey, I finally caught up with you," Samantha said as she came driving up in a golf cart.

Parker chuckled. "Where's your chauffeur?"

"Tor? He's back at Whisperwood. We do have horses to feed." Stopping the cart, she gestured for him to climb in. "Come on, I'll give you a ride the rest of the way. When I realized you were walking the course again, I borrowed this from the Canadians. They know how to do things right."

"Thanks. The second time around does seem a lot longer." Parker climbed in, grateful for the ride. Samantha handed him a bottle of cool water. He held it to his brow. "Is it getting hotter, or is it my imagination?"

"It's getting hotter," Samantha said as she drove through a grove of tall oaks. "The weather forecast predicts record highs for the rest of the week. That's going to take its toll on the horses, especially those from cooler climates."

"Foxy will be fine."

Samantha glanced over at him. She was silent for several seconds, as if studying him, but then she said, "Okay, so tell me what's been bothering you."

"Nothing's bothering me." Unscrewing the cap, Parker took a long drink.

Samantha steered the golf cart along the path, but her eyes stayed on him, and Parker knew he was going to have to give her some kind of answer.

"Okay, I guess I finally realized how tough the course is."

Samantha snorted. "That's not it. You love a challenge. Something else is eating you. And if you don't get it out of your system, you *will* screw things up."

"Gee, thanks for the vote of confidence," he said.

"Parker, you've been my student for what, four years now? And I know when your attitude is positive and when it stinks. And for some reason, since last night it really stinks."

Sighing, Parker capped the bottle. Reluctantly he told her about meeting his parents and overhearing Mark Donnelly and Jeff Steffen talking about buying Foxy.

"I'm glad I decided that I don't care what anyone else thinks," Parker said, his voice flat. "I'm going to show them all that I can win this event whether I have their support or not."

Instead of calling him a whiny brat, Samantha patted his hand. "I'm sorry about your parents," she said. "But you just can't let them get to you. However, I'd be thrilled to hear what Jeff said about Foxy. You made Foxy the wonderful horse she is, Parker. She was as wild as a rabbit when you first bought her. Sure, she's fast, and boy, can she jump, but the two of you were uncontrollable. Besides, no matter how much Jeff wants Foxy, he can't force you to sell her."

"True. But obviously he thinks *he's* got the expertise to take her to the Olympics and I don't."

"Parker, you and Foxy are a team. Remember that." Samantha stopped the cart, and Parker realized they were at the Old Mill, which was a new jump built to look like a mill. It had a steep, shingled roof and painted windows. At one end was a paddle wheel that spewed water into a stream.

"Captain Donnelly said there were two ways to negotiate the mill," Samantha pointed out. "You can jump the actual building, which is almost four feet high at the peak of the roof."

Parker eyed it.

"Or you can go around the mill, jump down a bank and into the stream, then up over a jump made of flour sacks," Samantha continued. "That way takes longer."

"Which is why most of the riders we walked the course with this morning are going the short way," Parker said.

"That's what Donnelly is advising, too."

Parker shrugged. "Fine. But I'll make my own decision," he said as he got out of the cart.

"That's your choice. But remember, Parker, it doesn't hurt to listen to other people's advice, too," Samantha said.

"I've got you and Tor. I don't need Captain Donnelly's help."

Quickly Parker headed toward the mill before Samantha could say anything else, but as he left he thought he heard her sigh.

"The judges are penalizing the horses for every little thing," Samantha told Parker late Friday afternoon. He was mounted on Foxy, dressed in spotless dressage finery and ready for his test.

The dressage phase, which was spread out over two days, was almost over. "Lyssa got a point taken off because Blue wrung his tail. Jeff was docked several points because Incredible fidgeted at the halt. They're taking off a lot of points for *little things*," she repeated nervously.

"I heard you," Parker said, trying not to sound annoyed. Samantha's hovering was making him antsy. Foxy was already wound up, flicking her ears and jigging nervously. Kaitlin had taken a long time braiding her mane that morning, and Foxy had grown irritable in the crossties.

I should have told her to forget it, Parker thought. But

Kaitlin had done such a good job, grooming the mare until she gleamed, that he didn't have the heart to say anything.

"I need to walk Foxy around before she bursts," Parker told Samantha. "And quit worrying. All we can do is our best."

"Right," Samantha said, forcing a smile as Parker rode around the practice ring. He let Foxy stretch out her neck, and he rolled his own shoulders, trying to get out the kinks. Samantha had every reason to be uptight. So far the highest score was 41.8. The previous year the top score had been 35.6. The judges were definitely being picky.

Besides that, fifty thousand spectators filled the packed stands, and it was boiling hot. Parker could feel the sweat rolling down his back under his black coat, and the band of his top hat felt like a vise.

Samantha waved from the entrance of the practice ring, signaling to Parker that he was on deck. Parker took a deep breath, pushing everything but the test from his mind, but he couldn't stop his pulse from racing. Foxy broke into a jig.

He laid his gloved palm on her damp neck. "Hey, girl, we're a team, remember? I know dressage isn't as much fun as cross-country, but we can still show the world that we've got what it takes."

Five minutes later they cantered straight down the

line into the middle of the arena. In the stands, the crowd buzzed with excitement, but as soon as Foxy halted squarely in the middle, the place grew dead quiet.

Taking off his top hat, Parker nodded sharply to the judges. Beneath him, Foxy quivered with suppressed excitement. Her ears were pricked tensely, and her neck was arched like a seahorse's, but she stood quietly, listening and waiting for his cue.

Good girl, Parker told her silently.

He signaled her with an imperceptible squeeze, and they took off at a working trot to the left.

Perfect circles, perfect beat.

Down the center line with a shoulder-in.

Balance, soft bend.

Half pass to the left. Half pass to the right.

Rhythm. Perfect crossing. Watch the bend.

Change rein at extended trot.

Show off that stride!

Halt and rein back four steps. Proceed in working canter.

Stand one beat. Count four back. Slick departure to canter.

Flying change at S. Extended canter.

Smooth change. Big, showy stride.

Down center line at canter. Halt. Salute.

Straight down the line. Hit the target. Smile.

As soon as they left the arena, Samantha, Tor, and

Kaitlin came running up with such huge grins that Parker knew he hadn't imagined it—the test had gone beautifully.

Jumping off Foxy, Parker gave her a Polo mint and an affectionate pat.

"She looked fantastic!" Kaitlin gushed. Lifting Foxy's head, she gave the mare a big kiss on the nose. "You looked just like a Grand Prix horse," she cooed.

Tor clapped Parker on the shoulder. "Couldn't have been smoother or more polished. You should be in the top five—unless the judges were blind."

"I could tell it was going to be a good test when we cantered in and halted," Parker said breathlessly. "Foxy knew she was onstage."

Minutes later he heard the announcer. "Moving into third place with a score of forty-two-point-two is American rider Parker Townsend on his horse, Foxglove."

"Yes!" Parker exclaimed. Then he glanced over at Samantha, who had stopped loosening Foxy's girth to listen. She stared at Parker, her mouth hanging open. For once, his trainer and friend was speechless.

Parker went over and gave her a hug. "Thanks for believing in me," he told her seriously. And when he stepped back, he could see tears glimmering in her eyes.

13

THE SUN WAS JUST RISING WHEN PARKER GREETED FOXY IN her stall. "Hard night again, girl?" he asked. He unbuckled her sheet, which was hanging sideways, and slid it off. The mare wasn't used to being in her stall all night, and Parker could tell by the mess that she'd been restless and fidgety.

Just like he'd been all night. It was Saturday morning, the day of the cross-country competition. Parker had barely slept. He'd woken early, grabbed a cold muffin from the kitchen, and driven to the park, beating even the grooms to the barn.

Which was fine with him. He wanted some time to think.

At the end of the dressage phase, he and Foxy were still in third place.

Third place, at Rolex. It was almost unbelievable. The night before, people who'd never spoken to him were offering congratulations. Lyssa, who was in fifth place, had been ecstatic for him. Jeff, who was in sixth, had nodded his approval. Even Captain Donnelly had offered a "well done."

Since dressage had never been Foxy's strongest phase, going into cross-country with a third place was a dream. Before, they'd always had to improve their weak score by riding cross-country with no penalties.

Still, Parker was afraid to get too confident. The riders who'd placed first and second were strong in all phases. Plus dressage was only the beginning, and he knew how easily horses who had done well in the first phase could still end up last after stadium jumping.

Stooping, Parker took off Foxy's wraps, then rubbed a mild bracer on her tendons. There was no puffiness or heat, good signs that Foxy would be in top shape for the grueling day, which tested both the horse's endurance and the rider's.

"Let's walk around and stretch your legs," he suggested as he led Foxy from the stall. She jigged down the aisle, her shod hooves clanging on the concrete. "There might even be a good spot to roll. We can't let Kaitlin get off too easily."

He walked her over the grounds to the stadium-jumping arena and let her look over the fence at the colorful course. Stadium jumping was the next day. The obstacles were big, tricky, and showy, and would be hard on the horses after the grueling endurance phase that morning. Parker hoped Foxy had enough fire left after cross-country to negotiate it.

Leading Foxy away, he circled around the trade fair tent and then headed back to the barn. The sun was up, and it was almost seven. Park workers were milling around, picking up trash, watering flowers, and getting ready for the crowds that would begin arriving at eight. Phase A of the cross-country, roads and tracks, started at nine.

Parker's head felt clear, and Foxy's stride was loose and relaxed. They were ready.

Now the barn bustled with activity. As he walked Foxy down the aisle, Samantha hurried toward him. Her hair was tousled, and dark circles ringed her eyes. Clearly, she hadn't slept well, either. "I've got good news and bad news," she said.

"Give me the good news first," Parker said as he hooked Foxy in crossties and started to brush her.

"Okay, the good news. The safety committee is adding an additional ten-minute rest stop after phase C of roads and tracks, and shortening the distance of A and C by three-quarters of a mile."

"That's the good news?" Parker asked.

"Yes. The bad news is that it's going to get up to ninety degrees today," Samantha explained. "That's why the committee made the changes."

Parker shrugged. "Well, Foxy's going early enough that the heat shouldn't be a problem. She's so fit, she could handle it even if they kept it longer." He dropped the brush in the grooming box. "Changing things only helps the competition."

Samantha rolled her eyes. "Okay, then for *you* the good news is it's going to be ridiculously hot, and all the other horses will faint from dehydration."

Parker burst out laughing. "There you go."

"No matter what you think, we need to watch Foxy carefully. Kaitlin doesn't have any experience with heat-related problems, so make sure you tell her what she needs to do. I'll make sure we have buckets of ice, a spray bottle of water . . ."

Parker nodded as Samantha listed necessary supplies, but his mind was elsewhere. He and Foxy were scheduled to start phase A of roads and tracks at nine-forty. Phase B, the steeplechase, was at ten, and phase C, the second roads and tracks, at seven minutes after ten. An extra ten-minute break meant that Parker would start cross-country at ten minutes after eleven, when it still wouldn't be too hot yet.

Foxy should be okay, he decided. Lyssa and Jeff

both rode before him, which gave them an extra advantage.

"I'll start getting all your gear together," Samantha said. She paused before leaving. "Let's discuss last-minute strategies before phase A."

"Right," Parker agreed.

He was picking out Foxy's hooves when Kaitlin came bustling in, eating a bagel from one of the concessions. "Sorry I'm late. I stayed out late with Jeff's grooms."

Parker chuckled. "Maybe they'll be so sleepy they'll forget to tighten Incredible's girth this morning and Jeff will fall off."

Kaitlin giggled. "That's mean."

Parker straightened. The blood had rushed to his head, and his cheeks felt flushed. He eyed the bagel, his stomach growling.

"I'll finish Foxy while you get something to eat," Kaitlin said as she popped the last bite in her mouth.

"Good idea." Parker handed her the hoof pick and started out. "Oh, by the way," he said before leaving, "Samantha says it's going to be hot. She needs to go over some things with you—what to do if Foxy gets overheated, stuff like that."

"Got it," Kaitlin said.

"And take good care of my girl while I'm gone,"

Parker added. "Make her pretty. Who knows, after today, she just might get her picture in the paper!"

Two hours later Parker pulled on his yellow knit shirt, black safety vest, and number pinny. Next he put on his medical armband and stopwatch. Above the watch he'd wrapped several strips of tape. On each strip he'd written the distance and time of the four separate phases with waterproof marker. In order to win, Parker couldn't afford *any* time penalties.

Kaitlin led Foxy over to his truck. The mare was tacked up in her cross-country gear—snaffle bit, dropped noseband, running martingale, galloping boots, bell boots, and hunt saddle. At the last minute Samantha had recommended a ventilator pad instead of Parker's usual fleece pad, suggesting that it would help Foxy stay cooler. Parker had declined. Call him superstitious, but he wanted to keep everything the same for this event. He hoped he wasn't making a mistake.

"She's ready," Kaitlin said, her voice tinged with anxiety. She wore a cap that said Lexington Feeds and smelled like sunblock. Earlier, a thin cloud layer had held down the heat, but now the sun was beaming brightly.

Parker chuckled as he strapped on his helmet. "You sound as though you were riding."

"I feel *worse* than when I ride. Once you start your course you're going to be too busy to be nervous. I have to worry through the whole thing."

"That must be why I feel so calm," Parker said, which was a lie. The bagel he'd eaten sat in his stomach like a lump of lead.

Taking Foxy's reins, he stroked her neck. With a toss of her head, the mare danced sideways. Her dark coat shone in the sun like polished mahogany.

"She looks terrific, Kaitlin. Thanks," Parker said appreciatively.

Kaitlin grinned happily at his compliment. Too happily.

"What's going on?" Parker asked.

"You'll see." Kaitlin nodded knowingly.

Parker shrugged, then checked his watch. "It's nine-fifteen. Ready?"

"Ready."

Ten minutes later they were at the starting area for the first phase. Parker was bent over, double-checking Foxy's boots, when he heard Christina's voice.

Startled, he twisted around. She was standing next to Kaitlin. When she saw Parker, she waved and smiled. She was dressed for the heat in shorts, a sleeveless top, a baseball cap, and sunglasses.

"Hey, what are you doing here?" Parker asked when she came over. Now he knew why Kaitlin had been grinning.

"I'm the number-one member of your fan club, remember?" Christina joked.

"You're the *only* member of my fan club. And I'm glad you're here to root for me," Parker replied. "I'm outnumbered by the big guns and their fans."

"That's not what I heard," Christina said. Lifting up her sunglasses, she set them on the top of her head. "Third place after dressage!"

"Number fifteen on deck!" the starter called.

"That's me." Parker glanced hesitantly at Christina. He knew she was here as a friend, and at the moment that was enough.

"Foxy looks great," Christina said.

"She *feels* great, too," Parker said. He looked over at the start box. "Well, I gotta go."

"Good luck," Christina said.

Parker mounted and a minute later was standing by the starter. Phase A was strictly a warm-up. Typically, Foxy liked to trot the 4.4 kilometers, which led to the steeplechase course. Fortunately, the ride was through tall oaks, which would provide shade. He needed her to arrive fresh and eager for the steeplechase.

The starter began the countdown, and Parker checked his watch. At zero, Foxy sprang into the air as

151

if she knew how to count, leaving Parker behind. He quickly regained his balance, reined her in, and settled her. The course was rolling, and the path curved right and left. Parker sat as lightly as possible and changed diagonals often. Every five hundred meters he stood in the stirrups and took his weight off Foxy's back. She pranced along, throwing her legs out in an extended trot whenever they passed a group of onlookers. When the finish line was in sight, Parker urged her into a canter, then hand-galloped the last hundred meters to get her pumped for the steeplechase. When they reached the finish, she was barely breathing hard.

Leaping off, Parker raised his stirrups, checked his girth and protective wraps, then remounted and kept her walking until his start time, which would be only a matter of minutes. The steeplechase course was shorter, 3.1 kilometers, roughly two and a third miles, but it contained nine jumps, mostly rails and banks topped with hedges, that had to be ridden fast. They had only five and a half minutes to get around the course.

Parker and Foxy loved the steeplechase. When the starter gave them the go-ahead, they took off at a gallop toward the first fence. Parker sat high, almost jockey style, inviting Foxy to take each fence boldly. She dove across them, her legs skimming the brushy top, then raced to the next. The second-to-last fence was the trickiest—a bullfinch, which was an overgrown hedge the horse had to jump through because of its height. There was a ditch on the takeoff side, and Parker steadied Foxy to make sure she saw it.

Leaving out a stride, she shot over the fence, stumbling when she landed. Parker sat quietly, balancing her with his seat and reins. Instantly she recovered. He checked the time, which was slightly fast, and pulled her up to an easier lope, taking the last jump smoothly.

When they reached the finish line, Parker continued Foxy at an easy lope. Phase C, which was over seven kilometers long, was designed to let the horse recover before the vet check and the grueling cross-country phase. It also took the longest time to get around—about fifty minutes. The start time was immediately after the steeplechase.

Parker continued to lope down the path, letting Foxy gradually wind down from her fast pace. Sweat tricked down his back under his safety vest.

Halfway through he slowed Foxy to a trot. Leaning forward, he felt her neck, which was soaked through. Since their time was good, he dismounted about a half mile from the finish line and walked her the rest of the way, giving her a much-needed break before cross-

153

country. By the time they reached the finish line, Foxy's breathing was steady and her chest was damp but cool.

Parker trotted Foxy into the vet box, where she was inspected and pronounced fit for phase D. "Her temperature's a little elevated," the veterinarian said. "But that's to be expected in this heat."

When Parker led Foxy out, Kaitlin and Samantha were waiting. Samantha had a worried look on her face.

"Don't look so gloomy. We're doing great," Parker assured her.

"I'm worried," Samantha admitted as she took off Foxy's saddle. "The heat and the course are taking their toll on the riders before you."

Parker grinned cockily. "Isn't that good news?"

Samantha narrowed her eyes. "Only if *you* don't succumb to the same problems."

While Parker kept Foxy circling, Kaitlin and Samantha walked with them. First they took off the mare's sweaty gear, then they washed her down from poll to tail. Parker sipped Gatorade and allowed Foxy sips of lukewarm water. When the mare was clean and towel-dried, they put on a fresh saddle pad, girth cover, and leg gear. Then Kaitlin greased the mare's chest and front legs.

The whole time, Samantha told Parker her concerns. "The first horse crashed at the Serpent and was eliminated. The second horse was retired because of heat exhaustion. Lyssa and Jeff just finished. I think they both did okay. Donnelly's talking to them to see if they have any tips on how the course is riding."

Just then Donnelly strode up with Lyssa in tow. Lyssa had taken off her helmet. Her dark hair was plastered against her head with sweat, and her face was bright red from the heat and exertion of her round.

"How'd Blue do?" Parker asked.

"Only one time penalty, but he tore the hide off his hind legs at the Old Mill. Fortunately, it was close enough to the end that we made it around, but—" Tears pricked her eyes, and Donnelly put an arm over her shoulder. "When we finished, blood was streaming down his back legs."

"Is he going to be all right?" Parker asked worriedly.

She nodded. "I hope so. Tony has him at the barn, and the vet's checking him. Anyway, Jeff had the same problem at the mill, too. Remember when we walked the course, we said we should jump the mill to save time?" She shook her head emphatically. "Don't do it. We found out the hard way that the roof of the mill makes a shadow in front of the jump. Blue totally misjudged the takeoff point."

"So did Incredible," Donnelly added. "He left out a

155

stride, hit the roof with his front feet, and almost fell over it. Fortunately, Jeff managed to stay on, but the stumble messed up his time and he had to push Incredible the last quarter-mile. They incurred a half a time penalty, and Incredible almost collapsed from the heat."

"Blue took off way early, too," Lyssa said. "But he hit it with his hind legs."

"So far, Lyssa and Jeff have the best scores," Donnelly said. "But neither horse will be at its best going into the stadium jumping tomorrow. My suggestion is to go the long way at the Old Mill—down the bank and over the flour sacks. It'll take longer and you'll have to go through water, but you can't risk a fall."

"Three minutes!" Samantha called.

Lyssa gave him a hug. Captain Donnelly slapped him on the back and then pulled him aside. "I know you're not a team rider, Parker, and I'm not your coach. But I've been watching you closely these past weeks. Now, I know you haven't always agreed with my advice, but—"

Parker swallowed hard. His pulse quickened.

This was when Donnelly was going to ask him to be on the team!

14

"I THINK YOU SHOULD LISTEN TO ME THIS TIME. YOU HAVE A tendency to ride fast. My advice is to keep Foxy at an easy pace," Donnelly continued. "Heat can be a powerful enemy on a course this size."

Parker's excitement fell along with his stomach. "Yes, sir," he said, trying to sound grateful, although his voice was heavy with disappointment. "Thank you for the advice, sir." Turning, Parker hurried toward Samantha.

His insides churned. Captain Donnelly was right about one thing—he *wasn't* Parker's coach. That meant Parker didn't have to listen to him.

"Two minutes!" Samantha called as she led Foxy over. The mare was jigging in circles, ready to go. Parker swung up on her back, barely gathering the reins before Foxy kicked out with both hind legs.

Kaitlin and Samantha stepped clear just in time.

"We'll see you at the finish line," Samantha said, frowning worriedly.

"Good luck!" Kaitlin cried.

Parker moved Foxy away from the crowds and toward the green Rolex sign. Trembling, she eyed it as if it were a fire-breathing dragon.

"Phase C was supposed to settle you down," Parker said, but he knew she was as eager as he was.

Taking the reins in one hand, he scratched her withers. The starter began the countdown. Parker legged Foxy into the box, keeping her turned toward the sign. When the starter reached one, he wheeled her around. At zero she sprang forward.

They were off, leaving Captain Donnelly, Kaitlin, Lyssa, and Samantha in a blur of motion.

The first three jumps were easy, designed to build confidence and settle the horse into a rhythm. Foxy rushed them as if they were steeplechase jumps, and Parker had to fight to slow her before fence four.

She shook her head, furious at the tight rein. Sitting deep, Parker used his voice and body, trying to get her into the softer, rounder frame they'd need to handle the trickier obstacles, but Foxy wanted to race.

She's just as stubborn as I am, Parker thought with a wry chuckle. *Fighting to get her own way.*

But he couldn't let her win this battle. Fence four, the wagon, wasn't technically difficult, but it was wide and high, requiring tremendous effort. He had to get her back in hand or she wouldn't have the impulsion to get over it. When Foxy saw the wagon, surrounded by a crowd of onlookers, she swerved sideways. Parker collected and straightened her. They had to meet the wagon just right to get over it safely.

Foxy rooted her head, objecting to Parker's aids. She took off when she wanted, which was too early, leaving Parker behind. He grabbed mane, trying not to throw her balance off, but her front hooves whacked the rim of the wagon bed. With a grunt of effort, she threw her hind legs sideways and twisted in midair, clearing the bed and landing without falling.

Gasping gratefully, Parker gathered his reins. The crowd cheered at Foxy's amazing recovery. She flicked her ears as if to say, *What happened back there?* then slowed. The near crash had made her check herself.

"You need to listen to me," Parker scolded as they headed for the Bridges, which required a sharp turn after the first element. This time, when Parker asked, Foxy softened and easily jumped the two bridges. Two obstacles later they reached the Porcupine, two hedges requiring a bounce, which Foxy again took smoothly.

By the time they reached the Head of the Lake,

Foxy's pace was steady. Lather flecked her neck, which was dark and slick with sweat. Parker hoped the water would help cool her off.

Cool them *both* off. Sweat rolled down his forehead and into his eyes. Reaching up, he wiped his face with his shirtsleeve. Then he checked his time. The Head of the Lake was halfway. He was a second behind the time he'd calculated, which meant he couldn't slacken his pace.

The crowd around the Head of the Lake was so huge, the ropes holding them off the course bulged. Parker scratched Foxy's mane, hoping to keep her attention on him and away from the noise and confusion. As they cantered the last few strides before the ditch, he pushed everything from his mind except the complex obstacle in front of him.

"You can do it," he whispered.

Foxy jumped the ditch onto the Normandy bank and leaped over the first set of rails. Ears pricked, she eyed the water skeptically, but she dove in bravely. Parker was glad they'd ridden Lexington Lake three weeks earlier.

Splash!

As they landed, cool water sprayed everywhere. Foxy forged gamely ahead. Loosening the rein, Parker let her trot to the first bank, then take one canter stride before the second bank. Foxy scrambled up, pulling herself onto the bank. Parker could hear her groan with the strain. Then she jumped the second set of birch rails and dropped down into the water again.

Chest deep, Foxy took two strides before jumping up onto the last bank and over the final oxer. Parker's chest was heaving. Rooting her head, she pulled the reins from his hand and snorted noisily. Froth flew from her mouth.

He checked his time. They had a few seconds to take a breather before the last half of the course.

Keeping off her back, he slowed her to an easy canter. She came back willingly. "You're half done, girl," Parker told her. "The worst is over."

Almost. They still had the Serpent and the Old Mill.

Six fences later they approached the Serpent. An ambulance was parked to one side. Parker caught a glimpse of a rider stretched on the gurney and a horse being walked nearby.

He took a shaky breath and tried to remember what Captain Donnelly had said about the Serpent when they were watching the video of the previous year's competition. Something about a false ground line that caused the horses to misjudge the takeoff point.

Parker leaned over Foxy's withers. "You've got to trust me on this one, Foxy," he whispered. "You've got to listen to me and not take off when you want to."

Her ears rotated as they cantered toward the stacked logs, which zigzagged across the path like a snake. Parker used his body to tell Foxy that he was in control. He squeezed with his legs and she obeyed, taking off at the very center of the in-jump. Land, turn, squeeze, take off. *Land, two strides, hold, hold, not yet, squeeze.* Foxy waited for Parker's cue, flying over the fence when he asked.

Hoots and cheers rose from the crowd.

"Yes!" Parker patted Foxy's neck as they cantered uphill. Her breathing was labored. He let the reins slide so she could stretch her neck. At the top of the hill he pulled her back to a trot, and they both took deep breaths.

One more tough one and they were home free.

Parker checked his watch, and his heart skipped a beat. They were behind time. Feeling his apprehension, Foxy broke into a canter. They flew down the hill, over the rails, and through the maze. The Old Mill was next.

As they approached it Parker eyed the building and its slanted roof. Again he glanced at his watch. The long way would take at least an extra ten seconds. Looking up, he realized the sun was almost overhead.

It's not angled enough to make a shadow.

Besides, Foxy had been listening to him. He'd

make sure she didn't misjudge the fence, as Blue and Incredible had.

Still, doubt nagged at him. Lyssa and Captain Donnelly had been adamant with their advice. But neither knew Foxy the way he did. She had the athletic ability to get over the mill even if they did misjudge it.

Besides, if Parker wanted to beat Jeff and Lyssa, he had to finish the course with zero penalties. And beating Jeff and Lyssa was the only way to win at Rolex or get Donnelly's attention.

"Let's go for it, girl."

Five strides from the mill, Parker collected Foxy. Two strides away, he spotted the shadow at the base of the mill. For a second he blinked, confused. Was it a shadow made by the roof, or was it the real ground line where the building met the grass?

Foxy couldn't wait for his decision. Leaving out a stride, she shot into the air. Parker grabbed mane, and his eyes widened. His mare was tired, and he could feel the strain of her effort. They weren't going to make it!

Up and up she flew. Her front hoof stepped on the point of the roof, and she used it to hurtle herself over the obstacle. Parker caught his breath when she landed and gamely kept galloping.

They'd made it!

Exhilaration filled him. Foxy took the last two fences without a hitch. As they rounded the corner Parker checked his time. Four seconds to go!

He leaned over Foxy's neck and squeezed his legs against her sides. Stretching out her neck, she flattened into a gallop. Parker pumped his hands like a jockey. He could hear the rush of air from her lungs. Captain Donnelly's advice about taking it easy flickered through his mind. He thought about Incredible almost collapsing because of the heat. But Jeff's horse wasn't used to the southern climate. Foxy would be fine.

A burst of applause filled his head as they galloped past the finish flag.

Their time was 13.02 on the button. They'd made it!

Samantha and Kaitlin ran up, tears rolling down both their faces. Parker jumped off Foxy and gave them both hugs. Grabbing the reins, Kaitlin led Foxy under the tree, where ice and buckets waited in the shade. Parker's legs wobbled, and he sagged wearily against a fence post.

Lyssa, Tony, and Captain Donnelly dashed up, offering congratulations and pats on the back. Christina ducked under the rope separating the crowd from the competitors and ran over. Wrapping her arms around his waist, she kissed his sweaty cheek. "I saw you at the Serpent and the Old Mill. You and Foxy were incredible!"

"So far you're the only one who's come in with no penalty points!" Lyssa chimed in excitedly. "That means you're in first place!"

Parker pulled off his helmet. His breath was coming in such ragged gasps that he couldn't reply. Resting his hands on his knees, he bent over, trying to catch his breath.

"Here, try this." Samantha handed him a towel she'd dipped in ice water. He scrubbed it over his face and neck, trying to cool off.

"You're the first rider to make it through the Serpent without a bobble," Captain Donnelly said. "Tony shot a video of it. Later we can study it and—"

Suddenly Samantha's panicky voice cut in. "Parker! Lyssa! *Everybody!* Get over here. *Now!*"

Parker swung around. Foxy was staggering as if she was drunk. Kaitlin was holding her, a look of horror on her face.

"What—?" Parker began as he ran over with the others.

But Samantha had no time for questions. "Tony, keep her head up," she ordered. "Donnelly, hold her tail. We can't let her fall!" She thrust a small bag of ice in Parker's arms. "Hold this on her neck artery. Kaitlin's gone to get Dr. Stein. Lyssa, you and I need to bathe her right side with cool water. Chris, you bathe the left. We've got to get her temperature down!"

Parker put the ice bag against Foxy's neck, but the mare swayed, crashing into him.

"Don't let her fall!" Samantha barked. Using their combined strength, Parker, Captain Donnelly, and Tony held Foxy on her feet, then propped themselves against her to keep her upright. Dr. Stein jogged from the crowd, pulling a needle and plastic bag filled with fluid from his medical kit as he ran.

Without a word he pushed past Parker, inserted the needle in Foxy's jugular vein, taped it to her neck, and began administering an IV of fluids, electrolytes, glucose, and phenylbutazone.

"Her ability to dissipate heat has shut down, sending blood to the brain," Dr. Stein explained tersely. Legs splayed, Foxy trembled violently as she took short, shallow breaths. "Her temperature's dangerously high, and she can't get oxygen into her lungs. I've got to get an oxygen tank."

"Will she be all right?" Parker asked, barely recognizing his own voice. "Please tell me she's going to be all right."

Without replying, Dr. Stein handed Parker the IV bag, then ran off in the direction of his truck. Sam took the ice bag from him and held it against the other side of Foxy's neck. "Don't worry, Parker. We're doing everything we can."

While they waited for Dr. Stein, Lyssa and

Christina continued bathing Foxy with cool water. The vet finally came back with an oxygen tank, and Parker helped him enclose the mare's nostrils with a breathing tube.

Then Parker stepped out of the way. Beside him, Kaitlin was crying. "I didn't know what to do," she sobbed.

"It's not your fault," Parker said, putting his arm around her.

It's mine.

He'd ignored everyone's advice. He'd pushed Foxy to her limit, and when she'd rallied, he'd asked her for even more. And Foxy, his wonderful horse, had given all she had—until there was nothing more to give.

And for what? Everybody already knew that Foxy was a winner. Parker had pushed her to prove that *he* was a winner.

And he'd done it. He'd made it around the hardest cross-country course in the United States—and he was in first place.

But when he looked at his brave and wonderful mare, her eyes closed and her sides heaving, Parker felt like the biggest loser in the world.

ALICE LEONHARDT has been horse-crazy since she was five years old. Her first pony was a pinto named Ted. When she got older, she joined Pony Club and rode in shows and rallies. Now she just rides her quarter horse, April, for fun. The author of more than thirty books for children, she still finds time to take care of two horses, two cats, two dogs, and two children, as well as teach at a community college.

Think You're the Ultimate Thoroughbred Fan?
Test Your Knowledge!

1) Which Triple Crown race(s) did Ashleigh's Wonder win?
> a) The Preakness and the Belmont
> b) The Preakness
> c) The Kentucky Derby and the Belmont
> d) The Kentucky Derby

2) What is Christina Reese's birthday?
> a) May 12
> b) December 25
> c) April 1
> d) July 4

3) Where did Ashleigh ride her first race, and what horse did she ride?
> a) Wonder at Churchill Downs
> b) Shining at Turfway
> c) Hawking at Keeneland
> d) Wonder at Keeneland

4) What was the name of Cindy McLean's high school boyfriend?
> a) Tor Nelson
> b) Max Smith
> c) Mike Reese
> d) Parker Townsend

5) What was the name of Wonder's last foal?
   - a) Wonder's Star
   - b) Wonder's Pride
   - c) Mr. Wonderful
   - d) Townsend Holly

6) Where is Melanie Graham from originally?
   - a) Texas
   - b) Kentucky
   - c) California
   - d) New York

7) Where did Samantha and Tor Nelson live before settling in Kentucky?
   - a) France
   - b) Ireland
   - c) Dubai
   - d) Holland

8) What type of riding did Christina Reese do before she started racing?
   - a) Fox hunting
   - b) Dressage
   - c) Eventing
   - d) Hunt-seat equitation

Answers: 1) c, 2) b, 3) c, 4) b, 5) a, 6) d, 7) b, 8) c

WIN!

A TRIP TO A KENTUCKY THOROUGHBRED FARM

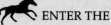 ENTER THE

THOROUGHBRED VISIT TO A KENTUCKY THOROUGHBRED HORSE FARM SWEEPSTAKES!

COMPLETE THIS ENTRY FORM • NO PURCHASE NECESSARY

NAME: _____

ADDRESS: _____

CITY: _____ STATE: _____ ZIP: _____

PHONE: _____ AGE: _____

MAIL TO: THOROUGHBRED VISIT TO A KENTUCKY THOROUGHBRED
HORSE FARM SWEEPSTAKES!
c/o HarperCollins, Attn.: Department AW
10 E. 53rd Street   New York, NY 10022

🔖 HarperEntertainment

17th Street Productions,
an Alloy Online, Inc., company

THOROUGHBRED 50 CONTEST RULES

OFFICIAL RULES

1. No purchase necessary.

2. To enter, complete the official entry form or hand print your name, address, and phone number along with the words "Thoroughbred Visit to a Kentucky Horse Farm Sweepstakes" on a 3"x 5" card and mail to: HarperCollins, Attn.: Department AW, 10 E. 53rd Street, New York, NY 10022. Entries must be received by June 1, 2002. Enter as often as you wish, but each entry must be mailed separately. One entry per envelope. No facsimiles accepted. Partially completed, illegible, or mechanically reproduced entries will not be accepted. Sponsors are not responsible for lost, late, mutilated, illegible, stolen, postage due, incomplete, or misdirected entries. All entries become the property of HarperCollins and will not be returned.

3. Sweepstakes open to all legal residents of the United States (excluding residents of Colorado and Rhode Island), who are between the ages of eight and sixteen by June 1, 2002, excluding employees and immediate family members of Harper-Collins, Alloy Online, Inc., or 17th Street Productions, an Alloy Online, Inc. company and their respective subsidiaries, and affiliates, officers, directors, shareholders, employees, agents, attorneys and other representatives (individually and collectively), and their respective parent companies, affiliates, subsidiaries, advertising, promotion and fulfillments agencies, and the persons with whom each of the above are domiciled. Offer void where prohibited or restricted.

4. Odds of winning depend on total number of entries received. Approximately 100,000 entry forms distributed. All prizes will be awarded. Winners will be ran-

domly drawn on or about June 15, 2002, by representatives of HarperCollins, whose decisions are final. Potential winners will be notified by mail and a parent or guardian of the potential winner will be required to sign and return an affadavit of eligibility and release of liability within 14 days of notification. Failure to return affadavit within time period will disqualify winner and another winner will be chosen. By acceptance of prize, winner consents to the use of his or her name, photographs, likeness, and personal information by HarperCollins, Alloy Online, Inc., and 17th Street Productions, an Alloy Online, Inc. company for publicity and advertising purposes without further compensation except where prohibited.

5. One (1) Grand Prize Winner will receive a visit to a Thoroughbred horse farm. HarperCollins reserves the right at its sole discretion to substitute another prize of equal or of greater value in the event prize is unavailable. All expenses not stated are the winner's sole expense.

6. HarperEntertainment will provide the contest winner and one parent or legal guardian with round-trip coach air transportation from major airport nearest winner to Lexington, Kentucky, visit to a Thoroughbred horse farm, and standard hotel accommodations for a two night stay. All additional expenses including taxes, meals, and incidentals are the responsibility of the prize winner. Approximate retail value $2,500.00. Airline, hotel, and other travel arrangements will be made by HarperCollins in its discretion. HarperCollins reserves the right to substitute a cash payment of $2,500.00 for the Grand Prize. Travel and use of hotel are at risk of winner and HarperCollins does not assume any liability. All travel arrangements will be made by HarperCollins. Trip must be taken by one year from the date prize is awarded; certain blackout dates may apply.

7. Only one prize will be awarded per individual, family, or household. Prizes are non-transferable and cannot be sold or redeemed for cash. No cash substitute is available except at the sole discretion of HarperCollins for reasons of prize unavailability. Any federal, state, or local taxes are the responsibility of the winner.

8. Additional terms: By participating, entrants agree a) to the official rules and decisions of the judges, which will be final in all respects; and b) to release, discharge, and hold harmless HarperCollins, Alloy Online, Inc., and 17th Street Productions, an Alloy Online, Inc. company and their affiliates, subsidiaries, and advertising promotion agencies from and against any and all liability or damages associated with acceptance, use, or misuse of any prize received in this sweepstakes.

9. To obtain the name of the winners, please send your request and a self-addressed stamped envelope (not required for residents of Vermont and Washington) to HarperCollins, Attn.: Department AW, 10 E. 53rd Street, New York, NY 10022.